MOONRISE F...

Vinod Kumar ...
Raipur, Chhatisg...
inner lives of or...
daily experience ... dreams, the mundane with the surreal. His first collection of poems *Lagbhag Jai Hind* was published in 1971, followed by *Vah Aadmi Chala Gaya Naya Garam Coat Pehankar Vichar Ki Tarah* in 1981. His first novel, *Naukar Ki Kameez,* was published in 1979 and made into a film by Mani Kaul. In 1999, Shukla was given a Sahitya Akademi award for his novel *Deewar Mein Ek Khidki Rehti Thi.* An English translation of Shukla's third novel *Khilega to Dekhenge* (1996) was published by HarperCollins India as *Once It Flowers* in 2015. *Hari Ghaas Ki Chhappar Vaali Jhopdi Aur Bauna Pahaad* was published in 2011. HarperCollins India have just published Shukla's latest novel *Yasi Rasa Ta* (2017) in the Hindi original.

Satti Khanna is Associate Professor at Duke University, where he teaches Indian Cinema and Modern Hindi Literature. He interprets the lives and works of contemporary Indian writers to an international audience through a series of documentary films and translations. He has translated Vinod Kumar Shukla's *Naukar ki Kameez* (*The Servant's Shirt*, 1999), and his novels *Deewar Mein Ek Khidki Rehti Thi* (*A Window Lived in a Wall*, 2005) and *Khilega to Dekhenge* (*Once It Flowers*, 2014). He has also translated Mohan Rakesh's *Akhiri Chattan Tak* (*To the Farthest Rock*, 2015) and Suryakant Tripathi Nirala's *Kulli Bhat* (*A Life Misspent*, 2016).

Moonrise from the Green Grass Roof

Vinod Kumar Shukla

TRANSLATED FROM THE HINDI BY SATTI KHANNA

HARPER ● PERENNIAL

NEW YORK • LONDON • TORONTO • SYDNEY • NEW DELHI

Published in India in 2017 by Harper Perennial
An imprint of HarperCollins *Publishers* India
A-75, Sector 57, Noida, Uttar Pradesh 201301, India
www.harpercollins.co.in

2 4 6 8 10 9 7 5 3 1

Copyright © Vinod Kumar Shukla 2017
Originally published as *Hari Ghaas Ki Chhappar Vaali Jhopdi Aur Bauna Pahaad* in 2011 by Rajkamal Prakashan, Delhi
Translation Copyright © Satti Khanna 2017
P.S. Section Copyright © Vinod Kumar Shukla, Satti Khanna 2017
Illustrations Copyright © Atanu Roy 2017
Originally appeared in Chakmak Magazine

P-ISBN: 978-93-5277-383-1
E-ISBN: 978-93-5277-384-8

This is a work of fiction and all characters and incidents described in this book are the product of the author's imagination. Any resemblance to actual persons, living or dead, is entirely coincidental.

Vinod Kumar Shukla asserts the moral right
to be identified as the author of this work.

All rights reserved. No part of this publication may be reproduced, stored in a retrieval system, or transmitted, in any form or by any means, electronic, mechanical, photocopying, recording or otherwise, without the prior permission of the publishers.

Typeset in 12.5/16 Adobe Text Pro
by Jojy Philip, New Delhi 110 015

Printed and bound at
Thomson Press (India) Ltd

1

Everyone
However small
Has an inner depth
That is deep
Inside one's own self
We keep tumbling
Topsy-turvy.
In that depth
Lies another world
Maybe opposite to the one outside
Sometimes one wants to stay a while.

One should stay.

We take notice of birds when we're children, less often when we grow up. We talk while we sit, we talk while we walk, we grumble when we're alone. We talk lying down. We talk in our sleep. But the patrangi bird talks only when it flies. It grows quiet upon alighting.

If it has something to say, it will fly. If it has nothing to say, it will perch. Patrangi. Sparrow-sized. Long tail narrowed to a point. Likes open fields. Can be spotted on fence posts and telephone wires. Noisy before settling down for the night. One flock finds a perch and falls silent. Another flock takes off with a ruckus.

It's wonderful to hear the bird talking while it flies. But it must get doubly tired—making sounds and flapping wings. So it doubles its resting—by staying still and staying silent.

There's a six-year-old in second grade. He wears a new earth-coloured shirt that'll look old the first time it's washed, and dusty-red shorts. He blends into the background when he walks across a muram field, disappearing from view before he has disappeared. Approaching from a muram field, he arrives suddenly as if transported by a zoom lens. He has dark, curly hair combed down in the back. He longs to fly. He gets lost in thought while he is seated somewhere. His mother calls out, 'Lost in thought?' as if she was calling him by name. He's known as Lost in Thought at school, too, though in the student register his name is listed as Bolu. He was called Bolu, or the Talkative One, from the chattering noises he made as a little baby.

It took a while for his mother to discover that Bolu talked only while he walked. He would stand still or sit down when he was silent. He learned to make intelligible sounds after he learned to walk. When he dragged himself on his belly, he could make 'cha' or 'ba' sounds. When he learned to crawl on hands and knees, he could say 'cha-cha' and 'ba-ba'. Luckily, he didn't talk in his sleep.

Because of Bolu's habit of speaking only when he walked, people wanting to listen were forced to walk alongside. His mother couldn't walk fast enough. Nor could she understand why she was tired all the time. Meanwhile, Bolu had figured out how to manage having to move while he spoke. When it was time to go to school, he pulled out a book from his book bag, and read aloud all the way to his seat in the classroom. He became quiet then either because he needed to sit down or because he wanted to keep sitting once he had taken his seat. On the return trip home, he read aloud in the same way. If someone asked a question, he stopped to listen. He resumed walking in order to respond. His mother knew he was almost home when she could hear his voice approaching. She would undo the latch and wait for him to walk in. Bolu got good grades because of his routine of reading lessons out loud.

His mother would serve him roti and milk but wouldn't ask questions; she was usually too tired to talk anyway. On this day, however, she asked him what they had done in school that morning. Bolu had finished his roti and milk and sat quiet. The walking and the talking had worn him out. But mothers want to talk to their children. Children want to talk to their mothers.

'Why don't you say something, Bolu?' his mother asked.

'I had a great time today,' Bolu said, getting up and starting to walk.

It was a one-room house. The door was ajar. 'The interesting thing was...'

Bolu said and stepped out the door. He knew his mother would follow. He kept walking as he spoke. His mother came out to listen.

'We saw a grey kitten in our classroom. Someone must have sneaked in the kitten in his book bag, and it must have crept out of the bag. My book has a lesson about a cat and a mouse. Could that cat's little one have climbed out of the lesson? How would it go back in? If a kitten came out of each person's book, there would be a pack of kittens in the classroom. They would look alike, many kittens born of the same cat in our lesson. How would I know which kitten was mine? The cat in my book knows who I am. I think she knows which textbook belongs to me. Its kitten would return to my bag first, to inside the book next, to the Cat and Mouse lesson last.' Bolu spoke in a rush and walked in a rush.

Bolu's mother fell behind with each word Bolu spoke. In the beginning, she fell behind a little. Then she fell behind one step for each word. 'Be quiet!' she called out to Bolu. Bolu stopped speaking and walking. 'Let's return,' she said.

'We've come a long way from home.'

'Yes, Mother,' Bolu said, turning around.

'Tell me what became of the kitten.'

'It ran this way and that. All the students ran after it. It was exciting.'

'Chaotic you mean?'

'No. A boy got frightened and started to cry. The boy standing next to him started to cry. The teacher noticed this contagion and began to laugh. The entire class burst out laughing with the teacher, even the two boys who had just been crying. I was busy chasing the kitten. "You won't get away from me," I called repeatedly as I ran after it. But neither I nor anyone else in the classroom succeeded in catching the kitten.' Bolu found himself close to where his mother was. He was about to say something else and step away when his mother took his hand in hers.

'Why don't you pause a moment?'

Bolu paused.

'Speak slowly,' his mother said. 'I'm tired. I'm holding on to you for support. I want to go home slowly.'

Bolu thought up a poem to make his mother happy.

> Patrangi! Patrangi bird!
> I will talk when I will walk,
> You will chirp when you will fly.
> Will there ever come a day,
> Mother, will you prophesy,
> When Patrangi and I will be
> Chirping, talking while we fly?

Bolu paused to hear his mother's reply. His mother hugged him to her breast and ran her fingers through his hair.

> You are still a young one, son.
> Go to school and learn to read.
> That is how your wings will grow.
> When they're fledged, you'll surely soar.

Bolu repeated his mother's words. He walked slowly, stopping for his mother now and then, committing his mother's words to memory. In this way, maintaining an easy pace, they arrived back at their house.

2

Bajrang Snack Shop was located directly opposite Bolu's house. It had been built long before there was a village—long before there were other houses. Only later did houses come up around the snack shop. Nobody knew why the snack shop was the first building. Some people thought Bajrang Snack Shop was originally a house and became a restaurant only gradually. The old-timers said it wasn't so. Indeed, there was nothing about the snack shop to suggest it had once been a house.

It served tea and snacks; that's all. The owner of the snack shop was called Bajrang Maharaj, whatever his real name might have been.

There was a cap Bajrang Maharaj liked to wear. It may have been white at one time but it was grime-coloured now. Even though it was washed every day it looked like it hadn't been washed in ages. The grime was colour-fast. Bajrang Maharaj had a pudgy twelve-year-old son. He, too, wore a grimy cap. The son had been made to repeat grades a few times and left off going to school. He helped with attending to customers at the snack shop, and spent his breaks trying to decipher a book of practical magic.

The school, called the Round School, was a distance away. The building was circular, as befitted the name. A wide verandah, into which individual classroom doors opened, ran around the entire building.

Not far from the Round School was another school called the Long School.

It was straight like a vertical line. When seen from above, the two schools made the number '10'. The long school had a long verandah in front and back. The back verandahs of both schools boasted wooden pillars.

The real name of Bajrang Maharaj's son was Bhaira. Everyone knew, though, that he would come to be called Bajrang Maharaj in time. The name 'Bhaira' was a corruption of the word 'bahra' for deaf. It wasn't that Bhaira was deaf; he was choosy about what he heard. If he didn't respond when people asked him a question multiple times, they assumed he was deaf. Then they would communicate by signs. Bhaira enjoyed this mode of communication. He never ignored a message communicated by signs. He would respond in kind. People who saw him expressing himself through gestures assumed he was dumb as well. Bhaira must have developed the power to ignore what was being said from the time he could understand words. He began to be called Bhaira while still a child.

Bhaira was afraid of speaking to his father in

words, but he felt safe using signs. Bajrang Maharaj knew that Bhaira would ignore his words so he, too, used signs. Bajrang Maharaj had the foulest temper. He would get angry at any little thing. People discovered by and by that he never got angry at messages conveyed by signs. So they began talking to him in signs. Sometimes they forgot and began speaking normally. Bajrang Maharaj would fly into a rage. If people resumed communicating by signs he would calm down. His attention would shift from rage to interpreting what people were signalling.

Communicating by signs was not possible when people were a great distance apart. If Bhaira was away somewhere, or hidden from view, Bajrang Maharaj would shout for him. On hearing Bajrang Maharaj shout, the tiger in the forest would roar back. The tiger seemed to recognize Bajrang Maharaj's voice.

Whenever Bhaira and Bolu met, the first thing Bhaira would say was: 'Don't speak. Let me tell you what I want to say.' Bolu would stand quietly till Bhaira had finished talking. Bhaira's last words would be: 'Speak to me by signs.' Bolu would stand still and communicate in signs. In this way Bhaira avoided exerting himself to keep pace with Bolu.

The outer walls of the Round School were smooth and shiny. The outer walls of classrooms opening to the verandah were smooth and shiny. The inner walls of the classrooms were different: they had built-in cubbies, starting waist-high and extending to the ceiling. The cubbies were deep because the outer walls were thick. They were of different sizes though, and a ladder was required to reach the ones that were higher up. The children would place their school bags in the cubbies they could reach, and take their seat on gunnysacks laid on the floor.

Bolu and Bhaira (back when Bhaira still attended school) were in different classrooms. When school was over, grey pigeons entered through the transom and alighted in the empty cubbies. They fluttered noisily like children assembling for class. They were careful not to leave droppings in the classrooms. Their uniform grey colour may have given rise to the practice of requiring uniforms for school children.

Sparrow hour came during the children's recitation period. The sparrows settled on doors and windowsills, filling the room with their chaffing. Swallows entered during any period they chose. They would make a rapid circuit of the room and fly out through an open door or window. They flew in and out so fast it wasn't swallows children saw but an afterimage of swallows. They weren't real; they were an illusion.

Bolu derived maximum benefit from the roundness of the verandah.

Guruji had permitted Bolu to go out onto the verandah as needed. Guruji and the other students would follow him as he began to answer a question put to him. They had a rule that all students listen carefully to responses other students gave. Sometimes Bolu's answer required only a single circuit of the verandah, sometimes more. On occasion, Bolu would be so absorbed in answering the question he would come down from the verandah and step onto the lawn, continuing to walk in a circle all the while. If kites or swallows happened to be wheeling in the sky at the same time, Bolu's wheeling on the lawn would have appeared to them just like their own.

The first time Bolu answered a question while walking along the verandah, Guruji said to him, 'Be more gentle and forceful.' Bolu was puzzled. How could he be gentle and forceful at the same time? Guruji explained that his pace was to be gentle and his voice forceful, so that those following behind had no trouble hearing him. Bolu began to speak in a louder voice. He didn't speak in a hurry; he didn't walk in a hurry. He composed his responses in short sentences, pausing appropriately at commas and full stops. He found a rhythm that matched words and walking. He avoided stuttering. He avoided stumbling. He spoke with precision, as if he was reading print. If he paused longer than usual at the end of sentences, it meant he was stepping from one paragraph to the next. His step was larger to match the paragraph break. Viewed from a distance, he and the children following him looked like participants in an education parade.

The Round School had a round perimeter. Before he left off coming to school, Bhaira was often punished by being made to walk along that perimeter. Bolu was assigned to walk beside him, coaching him in the day's lessons. Bhaira and Bolu were usually alone. The circuit was repeated many times; Bhaira would begin to drip with perspiration. Bolu would pause in his explanation so Bhaira could cool off.

'Teach me by signs,' Bhaira would say.

Bolu would try to explain concepts by signs, but it was useless. At the same time, he didn't want to tire Bhaira out.

※

Bolu was walking home one day, reciting his lesson to himself. He saw Bhaira walking towards him and stopped.

'Talk to me by signs, Bolu,' Bhaira requested.

'About what?' Bolu inquired using signs. People who have an alternative to communicating by signs find signs tedious.

Bhaira understood how Bolu felt. 'About anything except school,' Bhaira signalled.

A green pigeon alighted on a rooftop. Bolu spread his palms out and joined his thumbs together to indicate the bird. He pointed towards the roof. Just then a butterfly flew by between his hands and the bird on the roof.

'Butterfly!' Bhaira shouted.

'No,' said Bolu, taking two steps back.

Bhaira had failed to follow whatever it was Bolu wanted to say.

'You pointed to the butterfly,' Bhaira said.

'I pointed to the green pigeon on the roof.'

'A yellow butterfly was about to rest on the roof, but changed its mind and flew away. That's all I saw. I didn't see a green pigeon.'

'I didn't see the butterfly,' Bolu said.

Bhaira was only a step or two behind Bolu as they walked.

'If I had spotted the butterfly I would have fluttered two fingers like butterfly wings,' Bolu added.

Bolu stopped whenever Bhaira spoke. He walked while he responded.

'Friends should walk together,' Bolu said. 'You don't keep up with me.'

Bhaira had broken out in a sweat. He pulled the cap off his head and ran it over his face and neck.

They passed a house with a post in front for tethering cows. A patrangi bird sat on the post. The end of the patrangi's tail was thin as a line. Bhaira pointed to the bird. 'Is that a khanjan?'

'No. Patrangi.'

'Do you know the khanjan bird?'

'I do.'

Bhaira quickened his pace. 'I've been studying magic. A khanjan feather placed on top of the head makes people disappear.'

'What makes them reappear?' Bolu asked.

'Removing the feather,' Bhaira replied.

'Do people go somewhere when they disappear?'

'They don't have to go anywhere, though they are free to travel if they wish. Their presence or absence isn't known to others.'

'I won't travel when I disappear. I will stay where I am. I would have to speak in order to move. People would find out where I was if I spoke.'

'You'd still be invisible. I have a question for you: do you think I could bathe in the pond while I was invisible?' Bhaira asked.

'I don't know. You would become visible if the feather slipped off your head.'

'Does that mean I would drown?'

'Probably not, if you knew how to swim while you were visible. I have a question, too,' Bolu said. 'Can a snake still bite me if I am invisible?'

'I don't know. We'll know for sure only after we have become invisible,' Bhaira replied.

'I mean, a snake shouldn't be able to tell where we are if we have disappeared.'

'Bolu, I have a favour to ask. Teach me how to recognize a khanjan bird. I'll get you snacks from our snack shop.'

'Will you charge money for the snacks?'

Bhaira pulled off his cap to mop up more sweat. 'I am not tired yet,' he said. 'I have many things I want to talk about. I won't charge money for the snacks.'

'Will you kill the khanjan to obtain a feather?' Bolu asked.

'I won't kill the bird. I need a scorpion as well.'

'You'll have to look for scorpions under rocks. What's the scorpion for?'

'I need a scorpion stinger.'

'What'll you do with the stinger?'

'I'm not telling.'

'I'm not telling how to recognize the khanjan.'

They had come close to the Bajrang Snack Shop. 'Let's finish talking before we go in,' Bhaira said.

But Bajrang Maharaj had already smelled Bhaira's presence. 'Where did you disappear to?' he shouted. The tiger in the forest roared back. Bhaira panicked. 'One day I will disappear for good,' he said in a low voice.

※

An earthen stove was mounted under a roof cover just outside the shop. A wide verandah lay beyond, supplied with wooden benches and assorted tables.

The tables were rickety. If you set down a teacup the table trembled the way hot tea in a cup trembles when you blow on it. By the time the legs of the table stabilized, the tea would have cooled enough to sip. If a plate of snacks lay steady on the table, and you picked up a piece, the plate would shift position. If you reached for a second piece absentmindedly, you would miss your mark.

The benches were in the same rickety condition as the table. When you crossed your legs, you would slide down along the table to where your neighbour's plate lay. Glasses of water were not brought to the table; they would have tipped over the instant they were set down. Instead, water was placed by the rock intended for stepping onto the verandah. Customers would drink water on their way up, and set down empty glasses by the rock. They would do the same thing when leaving the shop. Bajrang Maharaj kept a sharp eye on the movement of his customers.

The verandah led to a small room. The dim light that entered the room seemed to apologize for being the little that was left over from the brightness outside. The room remained half-dark all day. A weak light bulb was turned on in the evening, chiefly to measure the extent of darkness in the room.

The light bulb was not turned on so long as the neon tube in the verandah stayed lit. Sometimes the neon tube stayed lit all night. These nights the verandah seemed from a distance like suddenly glimpsed illumination, promising safety to travellers stumbling around in a dark forest. Whatever illumination appeared in the Bajrang Snack Shop seemed also to have stumbled in there from the darkness. It was transient electricity, ready to be on its way out soon.

The rear of the snack shop faced south. For a short while after sunrise, a shaft of light penetrated the smoke rising from the freshly lit stove. The shaft of light signalled dawn. It was hard to tell—especially from the outside—where the shaft began and ended. The shaft of light seemed to be a clothesline to hang darkness on, after the darkness had been beaten clean.

The room stayed dark on cloudy days.

ॐ

Bajrang Maharaj ran the snack shop from a low chauki by the door. He would recline on the chauki with his head propped against a pillow so he could keep the verandah in view. It was dim where his chauki was positioned. The pillow was thick with grime, just like the dhoti and bandi he wore. If a person ran his nails along the pillow the scratch marks stayed.

The room with Bajrang Maharaj reclining by the door was a front for a cave. It was hard to discern how deep the cave extended. There may have been a wall at the far end. Or there may have been a tunnel, long and deep.

The back of the snack shop abutted an undersized mountain. There were large rocks in the back and smaller boulders scattered around as far as the eye could see. The mountain may not have been small to begin with. Big boulders may have broken off over time, leaving behind the present rock structure that came to be known as the pygmy mountain.

There was a hole near the top of the mountain. Cowherds would toss a stone in the hole to hear the stone travelling and hitting the bottom. The sound of its hitting the bottom could not be heard then and there. The journey down took a week. Seven days later—if one put one's ear to the ground and concentrated hard—one heard a sound like a stone dropping on a heap of coins. A person didn't have to return on the seventh day. The person could come back a month later, or a year later, or when they were old, and if they put their ear to the ground they would hear their stone landing on a pile of coins. Sooner than seven days, they would hear nothing. After seven days, a stone would continue falling until the person who had tossed it returned to listen.

The mountain was not high but it was deep. The mouth of the hole was wide enough for a person to enter. Not that anyone was known to have jumped in. Nor had anyone been known to exit from the hole. Even ants had not been seen crawling out.

※

After the Bajrang Snack Shop was built, people didn't know which house would be erected next. The people who lived in that next house were unaware when their house had been constructed. Most people did not recall when it was that they came to live where they lived now. The question of which house was the second to come up in the village remained unresolved.

The grass on the hut with the grass-top roof had grown luxuriantly for years. It did not wilt in the heat. When the wind blew, the grass bowed and provided an awning for the hut.

At the summer solstice, the sun would rise directly through the green grass. Right now, the only things coming up through the grass were small yellow flowers.

The villagers, and especially the schoolchildren, wondered why the Bajrang Snack Shop came to be when there was no settlement nearby. And, as far as people knew, the menu hadn't changed. It was tea and snacks when the shop opened and tea and snacks now. The shop's stove burned hard coal and its smoke could be seen from a great distance away.

In fact, all the houses in the village burned hard coal. The reason was the coalfield nearby. The villagers would go up to the coalfield and scrape off as much coal as they needed.

※

His father had told him, Bhaira said, that a squirrel was the shop's first customer.

'A squirrel?'

'It came for snacks,' Bolu guessed.

'No,' said Bhaira walking up to where Bolu stood with Binu, Premu and the girl, Koona. Koona was the youngest in the group. 'The squirrel came for tea.'

'Who was the second customer?' Binu asked. He stood the farthest away from Bolu. He had decided to imitate Bolu's style and spoke only while walking.

'The second customer was an elephant,' Bhaira said.

'An elephant!' Koona exclaimed.

'Must have needed a giant teacup,' Bolu said as he walked to where Koona stood. She took hold of his hand. 'Please don't say anything, Bolu. If you speak, you'll move away from me.'

'All right, I won't say anything,' Bolu said, and walked towards Premu as he spoke. Koona went and stood near Bolu again.

'The size of a bucket?' Premu wondered.

'The same as the teacup for others,' Bhaira said.

'With room at the top. Father says not to fill a cup to the top. Tea from the cup shouldn't spill into the saucer.'

'Do tigers come to the Bajrang Snack Shop for tea?' Koona asked while holding on to Bolu's hand.

'Why should a tiger bother? Even elephants are afraid of tigers. My father delivers the tea. He fills a kettle with four cups of tea and carries the kettle to the tiger's den. The tiger sips tea in its den. My father is grumpy when he sets out, but always cheerful when he gets back.' Bhaira walked as he spoke, the way Bolu walked. Everyone followed him to hear what he had to say. Koona slipped her hand out of Bolu's and joined the group listening to Bhaira. Only Bolu stayed where he was.

'He comes back alive. That's what makes him cheerful,' Bolu said walking towards Bhaira.

Koona nudged Premu to one side so she could stand next to Bolu once more.

'It must be true,' she said.

'Do you take tea?' Binu asked Bhaira.

'Father says I shouldn't.'

'How many cows does it take to supply milk for the tea?' Premu inquired.

'We aren't cowherds. We don't own cows.'

'Where do you get milk from?' Bolu asked.

Koona held on to the edge of Bolu's shirt and walked behind him. She stopped when Bolu paused.

'My father milks wild buffaloes,' Bhaira said a little too loudly.

'What did you just say?' Bolu asked turning to face Bhaira. Koona didn't expect the sudden movement. She fell but picked herself up without crying.

'Why would a wild buffalo let Bhaira's father milk her?' No one asked the question out loud though they all thought it.

Bhaira spoke on his own. 'The wild buffalo complies because it knows the milk is for the tiger.'

3

Some green grass sprouted on the ground not far from the hut with the grass-top roof. Both grasses were the same variety. It seemed as if the roof was beginning to sprout.

> The grass-top roof sprouts from mud on the ground.
> The mud walls grow from mud on the ground.
> Take care when you plant the windows and doors
> To name directions from the earth in the round.

Nobody saw the grass-top hut being built. Nobody saw the grass-top hut sprouting from the ground. Whoever saw it first saw the hut as already present, just as pygmy mountain and wide sky were present.

> What people saw was already made
> Earth and sky and forests and birds
> Rivers and seas and the animal world.
> The building of sun was hidden from view
> Of rocks and trees and rainclouds too
> Of flowers and springtime and night and day.
> May nature's blessings always stay.

A very old man and a very old woman lived in the hut with the grass-top roof. Small wildflowers grew amid the grass.

Once it grew dark, the moon moved out cautiously from the green grass roof. All the children knew where the moon lived. They could see the moon hiding behind the grass. The grass trembled and the air grew cold. The moonlight made the grass visible. People shivered partly from seeing the grass tremble, partly from the cold.

The children imagined they could touch the moon once they got up on the roof. They imagined they could catch a rainbow there and bring it down to play with.

At sunrise, the grass shone with coloured dewdrops. The new light was strung on blades of grass.

The couple that inhabited the hut had lived there for ages. Their hut, like huts of old people who had lived their days and nights with grace, was the site of a daily festival of sunrise and sunset.

The sun and the moon rose in beautifully different ways in every hut. The sun shone over the village like a diamond. The moon shone like topaz. Each new day was more beautiful than the last.

During class, children were free to sit in the cubbyholes if they wished. Their faces dotted the walls of the classroom while school was in session. A few cubbyholes were big enough for students as large as Bhaira. Some children dangled their feet from the cubbyhole and rested textbooks on their knees. Other children tucked their legs beneath them and rested textbooks on their laps.

The children would arrive at school freshly bathed, their hair combed neatly. The ones seated in the cubbies seemed to be ornaments brought in from home to beautify the classroom. Koona was too small to climb into a cubbyhole on her own; her friends would help her up. She always wanted to sit in the topmost cubbyhole.

Pegs had been hammered into the walls. Students could hoist themselves up to the topmost cubbyhole holding on to these pegs. They were fearless climbers. Students did not fall out of cubbyholes, but sometimes a book or a writing stick slipped from a student's hand. The children sitting on the floor would lean away to protect themselves, and the book or stick would fall without harming them. It may be that books, slates and writing sticks had become friends with gravity the way children thrown together during various activities become friends. Falling books, slates and sticks avoided children. They slowed down before they landed.

Sometimes a stick broke into pieces. The children used those pieces or other pieces in their pockets to write with. Perhaps broken writing sticks climbed the wall like caterpillars and found their way first into cubbyholes, and then into book bags. The school bag was their nest. It could also be that pigeons carried broken pieces of writing stick or erasers in their beaks and set them in the cubbyholes. Pieces of sticks and erasers were found in pigeon nests as well. The pigeons must have saved these things for their own squabs.

Bolu was the one who had initiated the practice of climbing into the cubbyholes. He started when Guruji was not around and continued when Guruji was present. His favourite cubbyhole was at the highest level, next to the transom. At this height, he was often out of Guruji's view. When Guruji thought to ask him a question, he took into consideration the excitement Bolu would cause climbing down to the floor peg by peg while his classmates cheered. Students in other cubbyholes would shift to one side to make room for Bolu's feet. The guruji from the adjacent classroom would come to find out what the commotion was. All the students from the adjacent classroom would follow him, Koona among them. She would clap her hands with joy. Koona would caution Bolu. 'Use those other cubbyholes to climb down.'

Guruji never saw Bolu descending. He would climb down behind where Guruji sat.

⁂

Guruji asked Bolu one day, 'How many days has it been since I posed a question to you?'

'It's been two days,' Bolu said taking four steps towards Guruji. 'No. I'm wrong. You asked me a question just now.' The students standing around moved aside so Bolu could walk as he spoke.

'When?' Guruji said in surprise.

'Isn't "How many days has it been since I posed a question to you?" a question?' Bolu asked respectfully.

'I'll ask you a question from the textbook tomorrow. Make sure to sit on the floor.'

'Yes, Guruji,' Bolu responded, moving back a couple of steps as he spoke.

The transom adjacent to Bolu's favourite cubbyhole opened to the roof.

The opening was large; Bolu found it easy to climb out. The wind blowing through the transom blew his hair back. He could smell basil from Binu's garden.

Sometimes he could smell wild mint from the forest mixed in with the basil. At other times, there was just the dense smell of dense forest.

It never surprised Bolu that swallows flew in and out through the transom. He thought of them as air—gusts of air made momentarily visible.

Students often hung their book bags on the pegs in the wall. Sparrows perched on the pegs and on the bags. The noise of their chirping accompanied the recitation of lessons. If a student forgot to take his bag home over a long weekend, he would return to find a sparrow nest under construction on the top of the bag.

5

As Bolu grew older, he discovered he had the sensation of floating as he walked and talked. While humming a song from the textbook he would sense himself borne along basil-scented air or wafted by air from the dense forest. At times, he was buoyed by the end of his mother's sari. At other times, he flew alongside the patrangi bird.

He recognized he was beginning to understand things. At an earlier time, he stood shoulder to shoulder with the student next to him. Now he stood higher than his fellow student. His feet were planted not on the ground, but in the air.

During morning prayers at school, Bolu would get lost praying for knowledge to unite human beings. He was exempted from singing the national anthem but he moved his lips and sang the words in his mind. At such times of enforced stillness, he longed to fly like a bird.

Bolu set out for the pygmy mountain one evening, humming to himself as he walked. The sun was about to set. From the top of the hill he could see vermillion colour spilling over the fields. He peered past the lip of the hole in the mountain. He thought he could make out milky light inside. Maybe the vermillion seeped in from somewhere below. He sniffed honey in the air. He could hear buzzing. Where could bees have made their hive? The hive wouldn't have lasted if formed along the route of falling stones. He wanted his friends know where the hive was. He waited for bees setting out to gather pollen. He waited for bees returning. There wasn't a bee in sight. Perhaps there was a thriving garden at the bottom of the hole and the bees didn't need to travel up above.

The pygmy mountain was easy to climb: it was the right height for children and the right height for adults.

There was a small Devi temple where the village ended and the forest began. The temple building had been constructed recently but the statue of the deity was old. There was also a beautiful pool adjacent to the temple, belonging to the same period as the statue. Stone steps ran around the pool to facilitate descent to the water. During the summer months, the pool was a popular drinking hole with antelope, deer, wild buffaloes and tigers.

A variety of turtles and fish lived in the pool. When a thirsty tiger came to drink, its glance may have fallen on a fat fish swimming about. It may have wanted to seize the large fish in its jaws. When a hungry tiger lay supine, its paws waving in the air, it may have wanted to seize a large bird as it flew across the sky. The tiger's desire for the airborne bird must be behind those statues of tigers with wings.

There were wrestling grounds, too, adjacent to the temple, where wrestling matches were held. There was a large round stone on the grounds used for weightlifting. Bhaira had gained experience lifting stones while looking for scorpions. He would be walking along and spot a stone. He would lift the stone. No scorpion. Disappointed, he would hurl the stone a good distance away. He was able to lift the large round stone in the wrestling grounds confidently, but he couldn't manage his own weight. Somebody would have to help him up.

One day, Bolu picked up a small round stone from the pygmy hill and tapped it against a rock. The stone broke in two the way coconuts break into halves. The inside of the stone was studded with blue quartz. Bolu laid down the two halves of the stone dirt side up so the quartz would be concealed. He wanted to tell his friends about the location, but forgot to afterwards.

It was a Tuesday. Guruji walked into the classroom. He announced that the lesson for the day was that there would be no lesson. The subject of the lesson was vacation day. He advised students to spend their vacation day well. When the class reassembled, he would ask them what they had done that day. They could spend the day alone, or spend the day with others as they did on a regular school day. They could use the day in their own home or gather in a classmate's home. If they were away from home, they would need to return home at their usual time.

'Will you spend the day with us, Guruji?' a chorus of voices addressed him.

'I won't be able to. The teachers are meeting to prepare tests. We will test you on your vacation day too.'

'I'll spend the day counting fish in the pond,' Binu said, though he knew it would be difficult to make a count of creatures that never stayed still.

'We'll play tag in the Devi temple,' some students said. Bolu and Koona, leaning out of their individual cubbyholes, were among them. Koona spoke out loud. Bolu indicated his wish to play tag by raising his hand.

'Did you say something?' Guruji asked.

'I want to play tag,' Bolu said, forgetting he was in a cubbyhole. He had been quick to right his error by grasping a peg with his right hand, and waving his legs while he hung from the peg. No one but Koona noticed. She was vigilant on Bolu's behalf, quick to warn him if there was danger.

She happened to be in Bolu's classroom on this day; she had forgotten to bring her writing stick and wanted to borrow Bolu's. It often happened that Koona's writing stick found its way into Bolu's bag, and Bolu's writing stick into Koona's bag. The sticks seemed to have minds of their own. They looked alike. The sticks themselves may have recognized differences in one another; it didn't appear that Bolu and Koona recognized these differences. In any case, Koona wanted to borrow Bolu's writing stick.

The students played tag. Bhaira couldn't run fast but he was in the game. Bolu stood on a pile of sand at one end of the wrestling grounds. He was lost in thought. Koona was It. Bhaira ran from her towards where Bolu stood on the sand pile. But running on sand wasn't easy. Koona was about to tag him when Bhaira pitched forward and collided with Bolu. Bolu stood lost in thought as before. Bhaira fell face forward. Bolu seemed unaffected by the contact with Bhaira. Bhaira received more bruises from colliding with Bolu than from hitting the ground. Koona and the other students helped Bhaira up. He was in tears. Bolu stood silent, lost in listening to birdsong coming from a maulsari tree. The singing bird was not visible.

Bhaira accused Bolu of pushing him. Koona and the others said that wasn't true. Bhaira had deliberately run into Bolu. The fault was Bhaira's.

'Nothing happened to Bolu. I'm the one who got hurt,' Bhaira sobbed.

'Keep your sobbing low,' Koona said. 'You'll get a smack if you start bawling. You are It now.' She mimed raising her hand to slap him.

'We will repeat the last round,' Bhaira said. He was playing the crybaby game; he didn't want to be It. At his plodding pace, he couldn't hope to tag any of the other players.

Koona knew she could catch Bhaira any time she wanted to.

'We'll repeat the last round,' Koona affirmed.

All the students, except Bhaira, went to where Bolu stood. Meanwhile, the bird had flown from the maulsari tree.

'Do you have bruises, Bolu?' Koona wondered.

'No. What made Bhaira fall?' Bolu walked up to Bhaira as he spoke.

'Didn't you get hurt from my running into you?' Bhaira asked.

'No.'

Bhaira seized Bolu's hand. 'Want to wrestle with me, Bolu?'

'No. I don't know how to wrestle,' Bolu answered, walking away from Bhaira.

'Afraid of me?'

'No,' Bolu said and took another step back.

'It's my turn to knock you down.'

Meanwhile, Bolu's attention had been drawn to an insect with gold and purple stripes down its back. He was lost in contemplating the insect. Bhaira rushed at him and tried to knock him down. Bolu wasn't affected by the attack. He didn't move from his position. But Bhaira's attack must have startled the insect; it scurried away towards a large rock. Koona began to sob. The other students grew frightened.

Bhaira walked away from Bolu. He wanted to build up speed before giving Bolu a shove. He couldn't believe it was he who had fallen when the two of them collided. Koona went and stood next to Bolu.

Bhaira moved away a few more steps. Then he charged Bolu, like a baby buffalo not quite steady on its feet. Sweat ran down his face. The sand from his fall clung to his body. Koona didn't understand why Bhaira was rushing towards them.

'Out of the way, Koona,' Bhaira shouted.

Koona stayed where she was.

'Move away,' Bolu said quietly, stepping forward so he stood in front of Koona.

Bhaira crashed against Bolu with full force. But Bolu had spotted the insect again. Light from the sun glinted on the insect's gold and purple back. Bolu was absorbed in the vision. Bhaira knocked against him and fell beyond the sand.

The fall hurt.

Bolu hadn't budged.

He lost track of the insect again.

He went over to Bhaira. 'Why are you crying, Bhaira? What happened to you?'

'As if you don't know what happened.'

'I don't know anything,' Bolu answered gently.

The other students gathered around. They had forgotten who started the trouble. They wanted to help Bhaira get up. But Bhaira hadn't forgotten who started the trouble. He knew. 'I didn't hurt you, did I?' he said to Bolu, groaning and smiling at the same time.

'You didn't hurt me.'

'Give me your hand,' Bhaira said. 'I want to go home.'

Everyone pulled together to haul Bhaira up.

'There's a lot of vacation day left,' Koona said, patting the dust off Bhaira's clothes.

Bhaira had tears in his eyes. The group headed back to the village.

They hadn't gone far when they noticed Bolu's voice was missing. He never walked with them without talking or humming to himself.

'Where's Bolu?' Bhaira asked.

The students looked around. They saw Bolu standing on the sand pile at the edge of the wrestling grounds.

'Come along, Bolu,' they shouted.

Bolu didn't hear them. A young man passed by Koona on his way to physical exercise in the wrestling grounds. She spoke to him. 'Bolu has fallen quiet, Brother,' she said. 'He isn't talking. He won't be able to go home unless he talks.'

The young man was new to the village. He didn't know Bolu. 'Do you need the child to be carried home? Please come with me and show me where his house is. I got to the village only last night.' He wanted to add that he had lost his way and was lucky to discover an inhabited village. But he thought the additional detail might be unnecessary.

The children accompanied the young man to the wrestling grounds. Bolu stood still as before, except for the wind ruffling his hair. The young man was strong. His foot knocked against the weightlifting stone. He raised it above his shoulders like a goalie and flung it to one side. The children watched in amazement as the stone bounced along the ground before rolling to a stop some distance away.

'Have you had a fight with someone? Are you hungry? Can I take you home?' The young man tried to pick Bolu up the way a careful adult lifts a child. Bolu didn't budge. The young man tried again, ready to lift a heavier weight this time. Bolu didn't budge. The other children made a circle around them. The young man took a deep breath. He exerted the full strength of his muscles. Bolu stayed glued to the spot.

The young man thought Bolu's legs might have sunk in the sand. He started to brush away the sand to free up Bolu's feet. The young man seemed agitated. Bolu could see what was going on but he was also lost in thought. He wasn't absent because he had vanished from the scene. He was absent because his mind was elsewhere. The young man began to pant from the effort to pry Bolu loose. He stepped away, eyes lowered from embarrassment over his failure. Bolu continued to stare ahead.

Bhaira smiled when the young man looked up again. He was glad to see someone else defeated by Bolu. Koona decided to run back to the village at this time. Bhaira saw her running and followed her. The young man did the same. Very soon the young man was at the head of the group. Who knows where Bhaira found the strength to run? He held his cap in his hand. It had fallen off when he had collided with Bolu the first time.

Bolu wasn't lost in thought when the students started running. 'Run together, run together! All of us, let's run together,' he sang. 'Double time is divine. Double time is sublime,' he sang. Sometimes his feet touched the ground as he ran, sometimes he trod on air. He took one step on the ground, four in the air.

When he was travelling through air, he sang: 'Fly along, fly along. Fly to keep up with my song.' The patrangi bird flew with Bolu while he was in the air, adding its chirping to his song. It sat on a branch when Bolu ran on the ground, waiting to fly when he began to fly. The patrangi bird was careful to avoid Bolu's streaming hair.

Running and flying in this way, Bolu caught up with his companions.

'Double time is divine. Double time is sublime.' Bhaira, who was lagging among the runners, heard Bolu's song first. 'It's Bolu,' he said. The others turned around and shouted 'Yes, it's Bolu!'

A group of people from the village approached them. Bolu's mother was in the group, as were the old man and woman who lived in the hut with the grass-top roof. The Bajrang Snack Shop cook was in the group; Bajrang Maharaj must have sent him to find out about Bhaira. The entire village was present except Bajrang Maharaj, and even if he had been present, nobody would have been able to recognize him. Bolu's mother looked worried. She had started a conversation with the young man. He must have told her about Bolu being stuck in the sand. The group wanted to pull Bolu out and bring him back to the village. Bolu's mother remembered the time Bolu was too small to turn over on his side. She could pick him up if he cried, but if he lay quiet she couldn't lift him. He would fall asleep on the floor. She would bend down to gather him in her arms and lay him on the bed. He was too heavy. 'He is fast asleep. I shouldn't disturb him,' Bolu's mother would think, and let him continue sleeping on the floor.

Mother and Bolu spotted one another. He took four steps in the air, the patrangi bird flying beside him, and reached his mother. 'Mother!' he cried. His mother picked him up and hugged him. He was light now, happy in her embrace.

'I'm hungry,' he said, kicking his feet as if he was throwing a tantrum.

'Let's get home first,' she responded.

Bolu had grown heavier as he became quiet. 'Sing the song of the forest air,' his mother said.

Bolu sang:

> The forest air makes a cozy swing,
> The smell of wild flowers enters my dreams.

He heard the patrangi bird chirping as he sang. He was in his mother's embrace but riding on air.

'Let me help carry Bolu home,' the very old man from the hut with the grass-top roof said to Bolu's mother.

Respectfully, Bolu's mother took the walking stick from the old man and set it down. Then she handed Bolu to him. The forest air had helped Bolu's mother lift him.

The old man didn't mind Bolu's weight. He seemed capable of bearing the weight of all the childhood in the world.

'Will you be able to handle his weight, Grandfather?' Bolu's mother asked.

'Of course,' the old man said in a voice that had travelled through human history from the first very old man.

They approached a house belonging to a very old woman. Bolu called her 'Grandma'. She was standing in front of her house.

The old man felt Bolu growing heavier. He set him down.

At the same time, Bolu's mother returned his walking stick to the old man.

'Grandma! Grandma!' Bolu cried as he leapt towards the old woman.

She was filled with motherly feeling. As Bolu hugged her, she ran her fingers through the curls in his hair.

Just then the wind picked up. Bolu disappeared from view. It happened in an instant. Bolu was right there but people were anxiously looking for him. 'Where did he go?' people wondered. Bolu knew that if he said he hadn't gone anywhere he would have to move away. Had a feather from a khanjan bird flying overhead landed on his curly hair? But there was a strong wind that would have blown away anything caught in his hair. Could it be that a khanjan bird was directly overhead? He looked up and there it was. He wanted the others to see the bird.

He moved from under the bird and became visible. The wind continued to blow. A gust bearing the scent of jasmine came to him from the left. A gust bearing the scent of dense forest came to him from the right. The gusts became wings in his sides. He bowed his head and rose in the air.

When Koona glanced up, she thought she saw Bolu flying. She could hear him say whoosh! whoosh! as he beat his wings. He was happy. Sometimes he didn't say whoosh! whoosh! and just glided along. At that moment, two khanjan birds flew over him. He disappeared from view. Koona heard Bolu say whoosh! whoosh! whoosh! loudly and beat his wings. He flew faster than the khanjan birds above him and became visible again.

Bolu was playing hide-and-seek. He would become visible when he moved out from under the khanjan birds. He would be lost to view when the birds flew over him. Four other khanjan birds had joined the first two. Bolu had to exert himself to fly away from under them. He lost track of time.

The people below continued talking about Bolu without realizing he was missing from the scene. Koona didn't forget and scanned the sky for sight of him. She thought she caught a glimpse of him once or twice.

By this time, Bolu had flown many circles over the village. He wanted to alight on the grass-top roof. He slowed the beat of his wind-gust wings and began to descend. He could see people returning to the village. The old ones were not in the party; they must be walking slowly, leaning on their staffs. The people who were present below seemed pleased with gusts of fresh air. They liked the smell of jasmine and wild foliage.

The grass on the roof was tall. Bolu parted the dew-laden grass with his hands. He wanted to protect the wildflowers as he landed. He spotted a rectangle of bare thatch and made his way there.

It got dark. His shirt and shorts were damp. He ought to go home. But he would have to beat his wings to fly home. That would make him colder than he was. Birds must not be affected by cold in the same way. Otherwise they would never fly through cold air.

The moon should be rising about now, Bolu thought. It would rise from near where he was. He would be able to touch the moon with his hand.

He was not a bird; he was cold. He descended gently. He saw the moon rising from the grass-top roof just after he landed on the ground. It was a harvest moon.

Nobody had seen Bolu land. He had a way of merging into the background that made him hard to detect. Light from the moon spread beauty all around. A piece of the harvest moon rose in each person's heart. It rose in Bolu's heart as well.

6

A customer placed a rupee note and a fifty-paisa coin in Bajrang Maharaj's left hand. Bajrang Maharaj transferred the coin to his right hand and dropped it into the cash box. The sound of a coin dropping among coins in the cash box was like the sound of rocks falling on coins at the bottom of the mountain.

The cash box rested adjacent to Bajrang Maharaj's chauki. Cash box and chauki were the same height. If the customer lingered after making payment, he could hear his coin drop in the box. It sounded as if the coin fell a long way. Its echo came from deep below. The customer might pause, puzzled by the far-off echo. Bajrang Maharaj would hurry him out by asking softly, 'Any reason you haven't left yet?' His softness sounded like a tiger's roar. The customer would rush away.

If a tiger roared while Bajrang Maharaj was silent, people thought it was Bajrang Maharaj speaking. They understood all roaring as Bajrang Maharaj's voice. If they didn't hear a tiger's roar for two or three days, they wondered why Bajrang Maharaj had grown quiet. People were also of the view that coins dropped into the cash box by Bajrang Maharaj travelled straight to the heap at the bottom of the mountain.

Sometimes a customer was careless and the coin dropped from his hand onto the floor. If the coin could not be found, the customer would reach for another coin in his pocket. 'Let it be,' Bajrang Maharaj would say. 'I found the coin.' The customer would leave in such haste he would hear the answering roar of the tiger only after he was a good distance from the snack shop.

It is likely that Bajrang Maharaj was able to locate the coin dropped on the floor. In any case, the clinking sound made it appear that the coin had dropped right into the cash box. There were people around who were afraid of paying Bajrang Maharaj directly. They would give money to one of their companions or to the man serving tea to pay on their behalf.

Sometimes, the man serving tea would say no and quietly signal the guest to drop the payment on the floor. The guest would comply. If the sound of the coins dropping wasn't loud, the guest would worry whether Bajrang Maharaj had heard the clink of payment. He would want to pick up the coin and drop it again. But Bajrang Maharaj would have located the coin while the guest was debating what to do next. By the time they looked down, guests were unable to find coins they had just dropped on the floor.

Nobody left without paying the bill. If people forgot and stepped out of the shop, they would turn around as soon as they remembered, climb up to the verandah and drop their payment on the floor. This procedure saved them from having to place the coins directly in Bajrang Maharaj's hand. Sometimes, customers didn't remember till long afterwards. If they remembered late in the evening or in their dream from which they awoke in the middle of the night, they would reach for their shirt hung on a hook. They would drop the requisite payment on their floor. Once they heard the ring of the coin on the floor they would turn over and go to sleep. If a neighbour heard the coin dropping, he understood this was late payment for tea and snacks at the Bajrang Snack Shop. If a coin dropped on the floor had no relation to payment owing to Bajrang Maharaj, the dropped coin could be spotted readily and picked up.

If a person couldn't find his dropped coin, it didn't mean that the coin had found its way to Bajrang Maharaj's cash box. Somebody else would have found it and taken it dutifully to the old man and woman, reporting the location where he had found the coin. He might say he found the coin in the lane of mangoes, directly below the tree with the tart mangoes.

Coins were the medium of exchange in the village. They didn't have to be local. Villagers found a way to use whatever coins strangers passing through brought with them. Only gold and silver coins disturbed monetary circulation. No one had coins enough to return change for a gold or a silver coin. If they did enter circulation, they were treated as common coins with gold or silver plating.

7

A hawk with pointy wings sat on a rock atop the pygmy mountain. The wings were blue and brown on the shoulder, white at the tip. The hawk was looking for prey. It noticed the two khanjan birds that had been playing hide-and-seek with Bolu.

As animals flee a forest once they discover the presence of a tiger, birds leave the tree on which a hawk alights. They fear the hawk's keen eyes. They fear the hawk's appetite. They fear for their lives. The hawk's eyes fixed on one of the two khanjan birds as it shot forward. For some reason, the hawk missed its aim. Perhaps the khanjan bird sensed the hawk's intention. Perhaps the other khanjan bird flew over the target bird and made it vanish. A khanjan bird can't disappear on its own—it lacks feathers on its head—but it can help with the disappearance of another.

The hawk climbed. This time it noticed the other khanjan bird. It shot towards the bird like an arrow. It missed its aim again. Perhaps the first khanjan made the second invisible. The hawk grew tired—not from the exertion of flight but from disappointment.

There was a stand of acacia trees between the village and the forest. It had been planted to keep villagers from straying into the dense woods. The tired hawk alighted on an acacia tree. No harm had come to Bolu's gust-wings when he flew through the acacia trees. Had the wings been made of inflated rubber, acacia thorns would have punctured them and Bolu would have dropped to the ground. But gusts of wind travel through acacia trees without trouble. The wind is puncture-proof. The hawk flew at the khanjan bird. Bolu couldn't see that the bird was being attacked. If Bolu had seen the hawk attacking the khanjan birds, he would have climbed higher and distracted the hawk. What was not seen was thought to have gone away.

Many people travelled along the path of the khanjan's flight. They must have become momentarily invisible as the bird flew directly overhead. Their disappearing and reappearing would happen in an instant. Not long enough for their companions to notice. One could stay invisible for a noticeable duration only if the khanjan hovered directly overhead for a while. It seemed simpler to a lay a khanjan feather on one's head for as long as one needed to be invisible.

The khanjan birds in the area must have begun to recognize Bolu and his friends. The birds wanted to play with them.

One day, Koona was going to school accompanied by her mother. Koona was walking briskly, taking quick small steps. Koona's mother was walking slowly, to keep pace with Koona. Koona was getting tired of walking fast; Koona's mother was getting tired of walking slowly.

'Walk fast,' Koona's mother urged.

'I am walking fast, Mother,' Koona said as she came to a halt. 'I can't keep up with you.'

'I'll slow down,' Koona's mother said, slowing her pace, but continuing to walk while Koona stayed behind.

Suddenly Koona sprinted hard, overtook her mother, and kept running till she reached the laburnum tree. She waited for her mother to draw near before she ran ahead of her mother again. Yellow laburnum flowers dangled by her ear.

Koona's mother picked up her pace. She kept her daughter in view. Then she looked again. Her daughter had vanished. Koona's mother thought she heard Koona say: 'These yellow flowers are fragrant' just before she disappeared.

At first, Koona's mother thought she had heard the entire sentence before Koona disappeared. Afterwards she thought Koona was visible as far as 'These yellow flowers…' The rest she heard only after Koona vanished. Or it may have been that she heard Koona's entire sentence after Koona was no longer visible. She panicked. Where could Koona be?

The khanjan bird settled on the laburnum branch above Koona. The flowers below stirred lightly.

Koona's mother feared Koona had gone into the woods. She broke into a run. In her worry over Koona, she ran right past her daughter, who stood under a cluster of laburnum flowers.

Koona, on the other hand, saw her mother running and felt happy. She didn't call out to her. 'Let her run ahead,' Koona thought. 'I'll sprint up to her in no time.' When her mother was well ahead, Koona shouted, 'Mother, I'm coming behind you.' Her mother turned and saw Koona. Her face lit up with joy. She had turned around immediately on hearing Koona's voice, but she had the impression that Koona was not visible immediately.

Koona had said, 'Mother, I'm coming behind you' while she stood under the tree. Then she began running.

It's clear that when we disappear we disappear from the view of others. But could it be that we disappear from ourselves as well? If we put our hands out when we've disappeared, will we be able to see them? Can two people who have disappeared see one another? Having disappeared, how would Bolu, Koona and their friends play hide-and-seek? They would have to hide behind what was visible to them in the disappeared condition, as say, a tree they could see, or a rock.

Koona could hide behind her visible mother. Even if an invisible Bolu hid behind a visible tiger,

Koona would be able to find out where he was. If she were invisible herself, she wouldn't be afraid of the tiger. She would be able to ride it fearlessly. Could she make her way to the bottom of the mountain while she had disappeared? Would she get hurt if she stumbled? Would she hear clinking if she hit the heap of coins? Would the clinking be soft or loud? Does a person who has disappeared have weight? Will the weight remain the same as before the disappearance? Or is there a rule: weight before disappearance + weight after disappearance = weight before disappearance? And an identity: weight after disappearance = weight before becoming visible?

Bolu may have become capable of descending into the hole in the mountain. As he grew older, he discovered that he became lighter or heavier if he hummed a tune. When he hummed sweetly, he grew lighter. When he paused, he grew heavier. He thought it might be possible to find the right balance for travelling down. He could also try growing smaller wind-gust wings. He would need to be careful going down, but might be able to enjoy full wingspan when he reached the bottom. The wind gusts at the bottom might be poisonous, though. He would choke. The plan would work only if pulses of fresh air from the top escorted him down.

8

There's a bird called hareva, green in colour, nightingale-sized. Different from the patrangi. Imitates the call of other birds. Usually travels in pairs or small groups. If spotted alone on a tree, its partner will be found on an adjacent tree. Hops from branch to branch. An acrobat in hopping. Green camouflage matches the green of trees. Blends with leaves. Its call suggests a conference of bulbul, kotyal, shaubeezi, kilkila, daiyaar and darzi – a conference in which each species is able to understand the language of the others.

There was an old stump near a tree. The hawk with pointy wings heard the chirping of many birds and alighted on the tree stump with its mate. Hawks hunt in pairs. One frightens birds into taking flight; the other pounces. The hareva sensed danger and flew away. Of the many birds the hawk had heard, not one was to be found on the tree. Meanwhile, the hareva was saved.

What the hareva's own call is nobody knows. The hareva seems to have forgotten its native language. Being a ventriloquist may be its only call.

The hareva sat alone on a tree. Many birds could be heard chirping together and Bolu was about to lose himself in birdsong. He thought he recognized the khanjan bird's call even though there was no khanjan bird in the tree. If there had been a khanjan bird present, it would have wanted to play hide-and-seek with Bolu. It would have hopped onto a branch above Bolu and made him invisible.

On the other hand, Bolu did have a friend a lot like the hareva bird. His name was Chhotu. Chhotu imitated the voices of his friends. Sometimes he spoke like Premu, sometimes like Bhaira or Bolu, sometimes like Koona. He hid behind a tree and called out to Bolu in Premu's voice. Bolu thought it was Premu. Just then he heard Bhaira calling him, 'Come this way, Bolu.'

'We are all here together,' Binu said.

'I am here too,' Koona added playfully.

'I am here too,' Chhotu said in no one's voice.

Bolu didn't recognize the speaker of the last sentence. Anybody would have had trouble recognizing Chhotu by his voice; Chhotu had been in the habit of speaking in the voice of others for a long time. When children were confused about the source of an utterance they considered the possibility that it was Chhotu speaking. But there was no confusion here. Why would somebody think of Chhotu when the voice was distinctly Premu's?

Bolu looked around. There were trees on every side. Somebody hiding behind one tree could move to the next without being detected. Bolu looked behind the tree next to him. No one there. He looked behind the next tree, and the next. After looking behind a dozen trees he concluded that his friends must be present but invisible.

He heard Premu's voice. 'I'm heading back.'

He heard Bhaira's voice. 'I'm heading back, too.'

'Me too,' he heard Koona say.

Bolu turned to look each time he heard a voice, but he saw no one going anywhere. He thought he saw a green shirtsleeve behind the karanj bush. It vanished when he looked again. Bolu advanced towards the bush anyway, speaking under his breath so he would not be detected. He found Chhotu hiding behind the bush. He assumed Koona and the others were nearby.

'Where's Premu?' Bolu asked.

'He went away,' Chhotu answered in Premu's voice.

'I heard Binu too.'

'Binu was here but he has gone back,' Chhotu said in Binu's voice.

The others were usually quiet when Chhotu was with them but sometimes they felt impelled to speak.

'I know you don't like to play with me,' Chhotu said in Koona's voice.

Koona knew what he said wasn't true. 'Everyone likes to play with me,' she responded.

'I'm speaking for myself,' Chhotu said in Binu's voice.

Binu spoke up. 'That's not true. Nobody refuses my offer to play.'

'Don't you understand I'm speaking for myself?' Chhotu said in Bhaira's voice.

Bhaira acquiesced. 'I'm slow-witted. It's true people don't enjoy playing with me.'

Then everyone including Chhotu said to Bhaira: 'We're your friends. We love playing with you!'

It was hard to tell whose voice Chhotu used when he joined in with the others. He might have thought that on such occasions he ought to contribute his individual voice.

'I was speaking for myself,' Bolu seemed to have said, but it was Chhotu speaking. Everyone turned to look at Bolu. He was seated on the ground. He hadn't moved while he spoke.

'We like playing with you, Chhotu,' Bolu said as he walked up to where Chhotu was.

Because of all these complications, Chhotu preferred to play by himself. He played freely when he played alone. He pretended all his friends were with him. He would speak to himself in the voice of his friends. People who couldn't see Chhotu was alone imagined an entire group of children at play.

While alone, Chhotu said in Binu's voice: 'Tell me Premu, what game shall we play today?'

'You decide,' Chhotu said in Premu's voice. 'You never say which game you like playing.'

'Let's ask Chhotu,' Binu's voice declared.

'What'll Chhotu say? He doesn't speak for himself, only on behalf of others.'

This was heard in Premu's voice.

'Binu, will you play with me or not?' Chhotu asked gently in Premu's voice.

A boy so gentle must be a wonderful person.

'I'm not playing with you,' Chhotu said roughly in Binu's voice. A boy so rude must be a terrible person.

'Why not?' Premu's voice asked.

'Because you aren't Premu. You're Chhotu.'

Koona's voice joined in. 'Binu's just teasing you. Of course, he'll play with you.'

That's how Chhotu played. His becoming quiet meant a lot of people stopped talking.

"You terrible Chinee," said Jo Pinaud, to me. "You know very which joke you like playing."

"Le criat Chinois," Billy's voice bellowed.

"What is this?" said Herb, as I woke in a heap on my bed of pines.

The room was full of mosquitoes.

"Here, said you may slain me or not," Chinin voiced genuine Pinaud voice.

A low expostulation. "Le peu voude of perme," said giant growl of a ... voice and one, till, an ... voice, "A low voudenne us be treated person."

"Why not?" Pepin's voice cried.

"Because you were to come." Said the Chinee.

Another roar voiced in. "I... I... but Pinaud von. Of course, Huff, you two are..."

That's how Chinee showed, and onought girl... mean afraid of me as you in a cabin.

People who came under the khanjan's flight vanished in the blink of an eye for the blink of an eye. There was no way of registering that they had disappeared and then reappeared. Nothing is visible when we shut our eyes, but the disappearance of something should be visible. We should be aware we are unable to see something we are capable of seeing if that thing is present. Keeping our eyes shut a long time is not the same as the disappearing of something for a long time. In disappearance, only that which has vanished is not seen; everything else is visible.

People who are blind see through their imagination. One blind person's imagined scene will not be the same as another blind person's imagined scene.

But people who have sight share the visible world. A person with eyesight sees a particular tree much the way another person with eyesight sees that tree. That disc which is known by one sighted person to be the moon is known to be the moon by another sighted person as well. Knowing the world by seeing it is one way. Knowing the world by not seeing it is another. One must draw close to something to be able to touch it. The blind live closest to creation, so close they can run their hands over it.

Children learned to know what they could see. They also learned to sense what they couldn't see. Blind man's buff taught them to sense where things were even with blindfolds on.

Koona had large eyes. Koona's mother said with pride that Koona's eyes were like a khanjan bird's. Koona couldn't understand why having eyes like a khanjan bird's should make them special. She agreed that blinking was like a wingbeat, and that the eyes could fly to something far away, but the eyes flying was not the same as the whole person taking flight. A bird could see something far away and fly to that something. Koona saw nothing when she closed her khanjan eyes. She couldn't see her hand before her face when she closed her eyes. She couldn't see her face in the mirror when she closed her eyes. When she shut her khanjan eyes, she disappeared.

While Bolu read his textbook on the way to class, his eyes saw little of what was around him. He was guided to the school by what he remembered seeing on earlier trips to the school. He knew he had to turn left by the banyan tree. If his eyes were on his book and he didn't look up at the banyan tree, he was guided by the tree's shadow. If he didn't notice the tree's shadow, he was aware of yellow leaves falling from the tree. In case of serious doubt, he would look back at the tree to confirm he had made the correct turn. Persons blind from birth have awareness of what they are unable to see. They also have awareness of what they have come to know by touch.

10

The village children wished to be in school even during vacation days. But they wanted classes to be conducted as if they were on vacation. The teachers wanted the students to tell them what to teach. They clapped and cheered if a student came up with a nice lesson plan.

Not everyone knew the story of Bhaira and Bolu on the wrestling grounds. Bolu would narrate a few details and forget to narrate other details. He also lacked knowledge of certain events in which he took part. These were events that occurred while he was lost in observing something. While narrating the wrestling grounds events, Bolu walked all the way to the wrestling grounds.

Koona wanted to be the one to add the details Bolu left out. She didn't like someone else completing the story. She didn't like it even when Bolu completed the story. She wanted to be the sole chronicler.

Bhaira had left off going to school on regular days, but he was faithful in attending vacation days. If vacation days were being held in school, he would come to school too.

Bhaira began describing what happened on the wrestling grounds. He wanted to suppress the part about his charging at Bolu, but Koona kept interrupting him, saying 'tell the whole truth'. So, he told the whole truth. It is possible he would have told the whole truth even if Koona had not prompted him.

When he had finished, Koona certified the veracity of Bhaira's account. 'He's telling the truth,' she said. When in her turn Koona described seeing Bolu flying in the sky, Guruji laughed out loud.

'Why are you laughing, Guruji?' Koona asked.

'Because I'm delighted with your report,' Guruji replied.

It was Binu's vacation day task to count fish in the temple pond. The task was difficult. Binu squatted on a partly submerged step, and began to count. The fish had already noticed either him or his reflection in the water. Their movement broke up his reflection. The fish weren't still even for a fraction of a second. They moved in and out of Binu's reflection. The count got confused. If he wasn't sure he counted them coming, he counted them going. He couldn't keep pace with their restlessness. The tally kept leaping and plunging like the fish.

He jumped up at one of the fish jumping out of the water. He lost his footing and slipped down the submerged steps as the fish dropped back into the pond. The fish weren't swimming: they were circling him, clamouring to be counted. They swam away, and swam towards him a second time. It wasn't fish food that drew them; they came back just to be counted again. Binu was sure all the fish in the earth's waters had entered the temple pond. They were innumerable. It would be simpler to try counting stars at night. He was tired. His clothes were wet. He had made mistakes. He had added a jumping frog to his count of fish. He felt hungry. He wanted to cry.

'Maybe my tally was not far off,' he thought as he headed home.

'Have you finished your vacation day lesson?' his father asked him.

'Yes, Father,' he answered.

He drew up water from the well to splash on his face. There was a small fish in the water bucket. 'One thousand eight hundred and thirty-nine!' he said aloud. He thought that if he drew up another bucket of water the count would go up to one thousand eight hundred and forty. The one thousand eight hundred and thirty-ninth fish swam about in the bucket. No. He was wrong. The additional fish belonged to the well, not to the pond. He tossed bucket and fish back into the well.

Usually vacation day classes were held away from the school. Koona asked her teacher whether it was possible to hold a vacation day class inside the school building.

'It's possible,' her teacher replied, 'but you'll have to do all the studying by yourself.'

The teacher began wondering how a vacation day at school might run. A school day at school started with the ringing of the gong, followed by prayers. The students then went off to individual classrooms with their book bags. No book bags would be required on vacation day. Which day would that be? Sunday was the weekly day off. Must vacation day be on Sunday then? Would children head for their individual classrooms or could they sit in one another's classrooms? And most important of all: what would they study? 'Think hard,' the teacher said to the children in his class. 'Think hard about what you would like to study on vacation day.'

'Whatever it is, we'll start first thing in the morning,' a student declared.

The students began to talk among themselves.

'Home in the morning or school in the morning?'

'School first thing in the morning.'

'We'll have to sleep in the school at night to start school first thing in the morning.'

'We'll have to bring our bed sheets and mattresses.'

'I sleep with Mother.'

'Then you'll have to bring her along.'

'Father is afraid to be alone in the house.'

'You'll have to bring Father along.'

'I have a cat.'

'The cat will have to come.'

'We have a cow and a calf. I'll bring both.'

'I'll bring my dog.'
'I'll bring my pot of tulsi.'
'Why the tulsi?'
'How else will it get watered in the morning?'
Their talk turned into singsong:

> One family has a dog
> Another has a cow
> Mine has dear old Grandpa
> There's Grandma in mine
> My house gets shade from ten whole trees
> There's shade from fifty in mine
> Shade from sixty trees in all—
> It's easy to combine.
> Grandpa, Grandma bless us all,
> Shelter like the shade of trees.
> May we your soft care receive
> Grow to be fine shady trees.

A girl sang:

> Make my home the holiday school.

A boy sang:

> Bajrang Snack Shop would be cool.

But there were students who didn't want to go to the Bajrang Snack Shop. They wanted class held on the grass-top roof.

'Can we sit there? Is the roof solid?'

'It's solid,' Bolu said. 'Just like the earth. Grass grows on the roof just as grass grows on the earth.'

The smaller children sang:

> To the grass-top roof we'll run.
> To study the moon and study the sun.

The first-graders sang:

> Sun and sky, sun and space
> All the Milky Way we'll trace
> Each planet we will study and know
> Then to clouds and rivers go—
> Then we'll study dams and bridges
> Kinds of dirt and rocks and ridges
> Slope-up hills and valleys low
> We'll study lions and tigers too—

One of the first-graders got frightened:

> Let's not enter forests wild
> Lions and tigers breathing near
> To a fat book let us go
> Read about tigers with nothing to fear.

The children split up into groups, talking to one another in song:

> Let's make friends with large black ants.
> Find their homes among wild plants
> Give them our home address.
> Welcome them with molasses.
> Let us play a novel game,
> Never ever played before.
> When that's done, let's play one more
> Game after new game galore.
> Countless novel games let's play
> Endless games for endless day.
> As many games as there are stars,
> Why does night go by so slow?
> Play the game of night and day
> Let the nighttime speed away
> So it's morning for our play.

A girl sang:

> I have thought of something new
> I will lead and you will follow
> I will get there first of all
> You will follow, short and tall.
> I will lead through snaking trail
> I will lead through swamp and brake
> All the dangers I will face,
> To get you there quick and safe.

Lessons were held in the school by day. Night was too dark. Night was the time to be home. The first people must have devised homes to feel safe in the dark. If there had been only day, the need for homes would have emerged much later.

Sleeping outdoors on rope beds in the summer, the children beheld a sky teeming with small lights. The forefathers had passed on knowledge about the heavens. The moon was the first light—bright and beautiful, its appearance changing each night. The elders in the family knew when and where the moon was likely to appear. The children watched with endless fascination as the moon slipped behind clouds or slid clear of them. The sky was a theatre playing mystery. The ratio of what was known to what obtained was nearly zero.

There were a hundred games the children played with the sky. Each question that arose in a child's mind was a game. 'Where is the moon?' they asked if they woke up in the middle of the night. They fell asleep once they found the moon. Sometimes they fell asleep before they found the moon. The moon and stars kept changing their place in the sky. The Big Dipper too. Only the Pole Star in the north stayed where it was, guiding all wayfarers in existence—a traffic policeman for those who knew their way already, and for those wandering on land or sea who sought it.

Guruji realized that the children wanted to bring their cows, dogs, cats, mothers, fathers and grandparents on both sides. An entire neighbourhood was ready to spend their children's vacation day at school and partake of their lessons. The announcement was silent, but even insects and birds heard the drumbeat of excitement in the village. Bajrang Maharaj got to know about vacation day because Bhaira told him. Bhaira was required to return to the Snack Shop each evening. He sought his father's permission to spend the evening before vacation day at the school.

The students agreed with Guruji that Tuesday would be a good day for vacation day. Everyone wanted to be at the school Monday night. It would be the night of the full moon. The Long School and the Round School boasted only a dim electric bulb, that had been further dimmed by coats of dirt and plaster.

Today was Friday. Guruji suggested they begin preparations for Monday night on Friday itself. The students stayed an extra two hours after classes, cleaning and sweeping around the school grounds. Guruji climbed up to the transom using pegs and cubbyholes, and stepped through the transom to the roof. Once on the roof, he unscrewed the light bulb from its post, wiped it and screwed it back on. The students below observed the care with which Guruji unscrewed and screwed on the bulb.

Bhaira stepped over the doorsill of the Bajrang

Snack Shop with bedroll tucked under his arm. Bajrang Maharaj swung his feet. This signified that Bajrang Maharaj was aware of Bhaira's presence. Bajrang Maharaj swung his feet again. This signified his asking what Bhaira wanted. Bhaira held out the bedroll. Bajrang Maharaj swung his feet. Bhaira understood Bajrang Maharaj's wish to know what the bedroll was for. Bhaira leaned his head over the bedroll to signify he wanted to sleep at the school. Bajrang Maharaj swung his feet faster and hit the cash box with his right hand. The coins inside jangled loudly. If the lid to the box had been open the coins would have flown out.

'Say in words what you want!' Bajrang Maharaj thundered. A tiger in the forest roared back. Bhaira dropped the bedroll from under his arm. The open jaws of a tiger flashed before him. 'I want to sleep over at the school,' he mumbled. 'They are going to be studying vacation day.'

Bajrang Maharaj tried to speak softly, 'But you've dropped out.' His roaring travelled to the forest. Bhaira heard deer fleeing in fear as the roaring chased after them. One baby deer couldn't run fast enough. 'Everybody needs to be at school for vacation day,' he said sobbing. 'Mother and Father, Grandpa and Grandma, tigers, lions, wolves, bears...' Bhaira wanted to say Bajrang Maharaj's presence was required at the school but he inserted 'lions, tigers, wolves and bears' where he should have said 'Bajrang Maharaj'. The sentence came out as: 'The presence of lions, tigers, wolves and bears was required at the school.' Bajrang Maharaj kept swinging his feet while Bhaira sobbed. The feet became still when the sobbing stopped.

Bhaira picked up his bedroll off the floor. Silently he asked his father's permission to go to school. Bajrang Maharaj swung his feet. Bhaira sensed that permission had been given. He wiped his tears. Only then did he notice that the snack shop was empty. There were plates of snacks on a table, and unfinished cups of tea. The tea had grown cold. The customers had fled.

As he headed towards the school, Bhaira noticed the cook from the snack shop hiding behind a rock. He noticed an older man and a fifteen-year-old boy, father and son probably, hiding behind another rock. They must have been the ones who had ordered the abandoned snacks.

Monday night was moonlit. The children had never before attended school at night. They didn't know how the school looked then. They were ready, waiting to set out. Uncles and grandfathers were still getting ready. A doll was being dressed up in trimming. Bolu saw his mother combing her hair and remembered Grandma. He was planning to run and greet her when his mother called, 'Time to do your hair.' He went to his mother. The process was slow; combing the curls right took a long time. He ran off the moment his mother's hold slackened. 'I am going to Grandma. I'll ask her to finish combing my hair.'

The moon was up. It seemed to have risen above the school and come over to the village to find out why the children hadn't reached the school yet. Or could it be that the moon had come to the village to accompany the villagers to school? The moon's silvery light made people eager. They felt they were delaying festivities by not being ready in time.

The moon had risen from the grass of the green roof. Its light was wet with dew. A cool wind, damp from the moonlight, flowed over the village. The children shouted noisily. Hearing their clamour a stranger could be excused for imagining only children inhabited this village. If he rapped on one door, a girl dressed like a bride would answer the door. If he rapped on another, a boy dressed like a groom would answer the door. 'Have you lost your way?' the boy would ask. The visitor would imagine he looked lost because he was grown-up. A stranger child rapping on the door would not seem to have lost his way.

The children were about to leave. The moon stood on tiptoe, peeping through the windows. The wind stopped, the better to see children coming out onto the street. The wind stopped, it's true, but tree branches continued to wave and leaves to flutter. They were excited to be near the children.

The first child appeared on the street with his mother, like the first flower in a garden. 'The others have left already,' he complained to his mother. 'Yes,' his mother said. Just then the other children emerged from their houses saying, 'We are here!' The street was filled with flowers. A cavalcade of children and parents and elders was on its way to a festival. The moon lit their path. Bolu thought the moon travelled with him. Koona rode on a pony that she wasn't tall enough to mount on her own. She had been helped up. Koona, too, thought the moon travelled with her. Each person in that cavalcade thought similarly. Indeed the moon was with them all, leaving no one behind.

Bolu hummed a song. There was music in the air already, borne along the light of the moon. The leaves fluttered. Their fluttering did not have the usual effect of deepening the silence of the night. Instead, the fluttering lightened the silence, making it musical. Cows and buffaloes were part of the cavalcade, the tun-tun-tun of their bells adding to the music in the air.

The school gong sounded eight times. The gong rebuked the children for being tardy. It was late for them; normally they would be in bed by this time. But enthusiasm for sleeping at the school kept them awake. It would have been better for their daily routine if they had gotten to school by six-thirty or seven in the evening. The elders urged the children to hurry; some of the children in the cavalcade broke into a run.

Koona called out to Bolu as her pony approached him on the road. 'It's getting late, Bolu. Why don't you ride with me on my pony?'

'Thanks,' Bolu said. 'I'll ride my own pony.'

'Where's the pony?'

Bolu's pony was ready. He quickened his pace until he was running.

He began humming to himself and his body grew lighter. Wind-gust wings extended from his right and left shoulders. The skies became a book he could read, the moon was the dot on the i. He wanted to fly up to the moon but then he remembered school. With two wing beats he came close to Koona on her pony. He whispered her name. He was already past her when she looked up. 'I'll get to school ahead of you,' he said.

Koona was bewildered by the magic trick she saw. Her pony was equally bewildered and slowed down. Koona pressed with her little heels to make it go faster. She called out to Bolu, 'Can I ride on your pony? It's better than mine. The least you can do is let me ride ahead of you.'

'Let's travel together, neither of us ahead of the other,' Bolu responded.

'Shall I get on your pony?'

'My pony won't be able to take your weight.'

'Is your pony starving?'

'No, it's you who is fat. The pony won't be able to carry the weight of two,' Bolu said extending his right hand to Koona. Bolu moved away from Koona's pony and for a little while he and Koona flew together in the air, Koona holding Bolu's hand. But Bolu was being dragged down by Koona's weight. He could maintain only a pony's height above the ground. When they passed a rock, Koona tucked her knees in to avoid being scraped by the rock. There were trees ahead. Bolu tried, but failed to lighten himself so they could rise above the trees. He stopped his humming and grew heavier. Koona was able to step down onto the ground.

Her pony had run on ahead. She remembered the pony only when she was back on earth. Now her worries about the pony made her forget she had just been flying.

The school drew near. Bolu and Koona paused as they entered the school grounds. The classrooms looked poorly lit. Reading would have been impossible in the faint light. Fortunately, this was not a reading and writing kind of day.

The moon hung in the open sky like a bulb, in

fact, like a floodlight. It was the eve of their vacation day. Children and parents were about to arrive. Conversation among approaching pupils had become audible. Or could it be Chhotu alone carrying on a conversation in his many voices? If Chhotu assumed the voice of Bajrang Maharaj, would a tiger roar back in response? It couldn't be that everyone would be taken in by Chhotu's voices. The tiger must know which voice belonged to the real Bajrang Maharaj.

The sky was thick with stars. Perhaps the stars attended school at night.

This night it was the children attending school. The stars vacated the classrooms for the children and packed the sky. They were the questions children wanted to ask, but had never asked out loud. Now they glowed in the firmament so someone would deliver the answers directly into the hearts of children.

Bhaira was among the students flocking to the school. He looked this way and that but couldn't locate Bolu. He hung back, hoping to find Bolu at the rear of the group, and got separated from the others. The moon was shining, but there were pockets the moon could not reach. Bhaira held on tight to his bedroll. Some people walked by. He heard his own voice saying, 'Will Koona be staying away from school, Bolu?' That's the question he would have asked if he had met Bolu and noticed Koona was not with him. But Bhaira hadn't spoken and he hadn't found Bolu.

Had his thoughts expressed themselves out loud on their own? In any case, there was no Bolu around to whom the imagined question might have been addressed.

'Why don't you answer, Bolu?' Bhaira heard Bhaira asking.

'I am Bhaira, Bolu,' Bhaira shouted out. 'Where are you?'

He heard Bhaira saying, 'Chhotu seems to be imitating Bhaira's voice and making fools of us.'

Bhaira turned to the source of the voice. It was dark there because of trees. He moved rapidly, parting bushes to make a path.

'It's me, Bolu,' he said. 'I've been looking for you.'

'You can't be Bhaira. Bhaira is walking beside me,' Bolu said. 'Are you Chhotu or are you some magician?'

'It's me, Bolu. Don't be misled by whoever says he is Bhaira. I'm on my way to school. I've been looking for all of you a long time. The person with you is a magician pretending to be me. Or else you are both playing tricks on me.'

'It's you who are playing tricks. Bhaira is with me. Tell me your real name,' he heard Bolu say.

'Bhaira is my real name,' Bhaira said.

The darkness found gloomy places to lurk in and pounced on a person unawares. These places were gloomy because no one cared to visit them. While looking for Bolu, Bhaira lurched close to a dangerous pit. He recovered his balance just in time. Had he fallen in, it would have been difficult to pull him out. The moon had already fallen into the rainwater at the bottom of the pit, and it wasn't clear how the moon could be pulled out.

The pit kept growing deeper day by day. It was the only place nearby for muram soil. People had made steps down the side of the pit to get to the muram at the base. The steps went lower and lower as the muram was dug out. Some of the steps had collapsed; it was dangerous to climb down. Bhaira had been able to steady himself but he couldn't hold on to the bedroll. It rolled away from him down the side of the pit, stopping just short of the water at the bottom. 'Bolu,' he shouted. 'My bedroll has fallen into the pit. Help me, please. I'm entering the pit to see if I can get it out.'

'Don't go into the pit. We're on our way to help you.' That was Bolu's voice.

'Hold on. I'm coming too.' That was Koona's voice.

Bhaira had been out of practice in ignoring what people said to him. He resumed that practice now. He went down one step at a time. The shadow of branches played on the steps and disturbed estimation of depth, the way bifocal lenses disturb estimation of depth as a person descends a staircase.

He heard Binu's voice. 'This is Chhotu speaking. I'm with the group too.'

'You are Binu,' Bhaira said.

Chhotu knew the art of making other people seem to be present by imitating their voices. He didn't know the art of making himself known to be present by using his own voice.

'This is Chhotu speaking. I'm alone. There's just me,' he said in Bolu's voice.

'You are Bolu,' Bhaira said.

'I promise it's me. I'm Chhotu,' he said in Koona's voice.

Bhaira was confused. Was it Chhotu teasing him or was it Koona? He glanced up and saw someone who resembled Chhotu.

Bhaira had gone down three steps by now. On the fourth his foot hit a corner, causing the step to collapse. He fell but was saved from serious harm by landing in the water below. He skinned his hands, that was all.

He looked around and felt less lonely on seeing the moon in the water. Then a cloud hid the moon, covering the water with a layer of white. Where did the moon go? Bhaira felt like crying. He could hear rustling nearby. The moon in the sky couldn't have heard the rustling, but perhaps the moon in the water had. It stuck its head out from behind the layer of white. If it was the moon's reflection below, the moon was the reflection's moon above. It, too, slipped out from behind clouds.

Bhaira thought he saw a jackal at the rim of the pit. He imagined Chhotu had run to tell the others about his fall. Chhotu may have tried to find Bolu. Better if he didn't let Bajrang Maharaj know. There was no way to climb back up. The step that collapsed had destroyed the two steps below it. He would have to spend the night in the pit. He was sorry not to have made it to the school.

His bedroll consisted of a thin rug and a bed sheet. His body wanted sleep, but fear kept him awake. An elephant could have dropped into the pit just as he had. If he wasn't crushed by the falling elephant, he could scramble onto the elephant's back and get out of the pit that way. But why would a wild elephant let him ride on its back? He'd be picked up by the trunk and dashed to pieces on the ground. A tame elephant would have wrapped its trunk around Bhaira and helped him up. Tame elephants are bright, too bright to fall into a pit. The elephant that fell in would have to be as stupid as Bhaira was.

He glanced up. The jackal was still there. Its eyes flashed, lit by the moon in the water. It circled the pit, seeking a safe route down.

Bhaira laid the rug next to the muram wall and wrapped the sheet around him. It was cold. He was being bitten by mosquitoes. He wanted to prop himself against the wall. He saw some rocks lying nearby and began to gather them for self-protection. The first large rock he picked up had three scorpions under it. They skittered away to new hiding places. He had never uncovered scorpions before.

A tiger roared. It roared so loud that chunks of muram adhering to the walls of the pit shook loose and tumbled into the water. The jackal scampered away. Perhaps Bajrang Maharaj had called out 'BHAIRA!' and the tiger roared back 'BHAIRA!' If Bhaira said 'Father!' would the tiger roar back 'Father!'?

'Father!' Bhaira shouted. He heard a tiger cub growling from very near. A single chunk of muram shook loose and tumbled into the water.

Chhotu had rushed to the village to report that Bhaira had fallen in the pit. The village was empty. He ran towards the school. He saw the snack-maker walking ahead of him, a big flashlight in his hand. 'Stop please and listen to me. Bhaira has fallen into the muram pit,' Chhotu said to the snack-maker. He was out of breath. The voice he spoke in was Bhaira's.

The snack-maker was not one to stop at anyone's bidding. Besides, Bajrang Maharaj may have told him not to be diverted from his mission. The voice he heard confused him. 'Bhaira?' he asked. But the person before him was not Bhaira; it was just a small-sized boy. Out of his own worries for Bhaira he may have imagined it was Bhaira's voice he heard. 'I know about Bhaira,' he said, resuming his brisk pace.

'How did you find out?' Chhotu asked in Bolu's voice.

'Who just spoke?' the snack-maker was baffled. He could see only the small-sized boy who had asked him to stop. He didn't want to answer the question posed to him, but in his confusion, blurted out 'Bajrang Maharaj told me.' Saying this, he broke into a run.

'How did Bajrang Maharaj know?' the snack-maker heard a girl's voice asking him. It was Koona's voice he heard but he didn't know Koona. 'Where did this little girl come from?' he wondered. He looked back and saw only the small-sized boy. He pointed his flashlight at the boy's face. It was a nice-looking face.

The flashlight beam caught Chhotu's eyes. He was irritated. 'What's going on?' he asked in Bajrang Maharaj's voice. 'Go and find Bhaira.' Tigers began to roar as he spoke. They didn't seem to be far away.

Ordinarily, the snack-maker would have hurried to safety when he heard tigers, but he had to obey Bajrang Maharaj's instructions. He ran anxiously towards the muram pit. The flashlight in his hand cast a wobbly light. Whatever the light fell on seemed to be trembling—rocks, trees, an isolated hut, the wide earth. Had the beam of his flashlight reached the sky, the sky too would have quaked in fear.

11

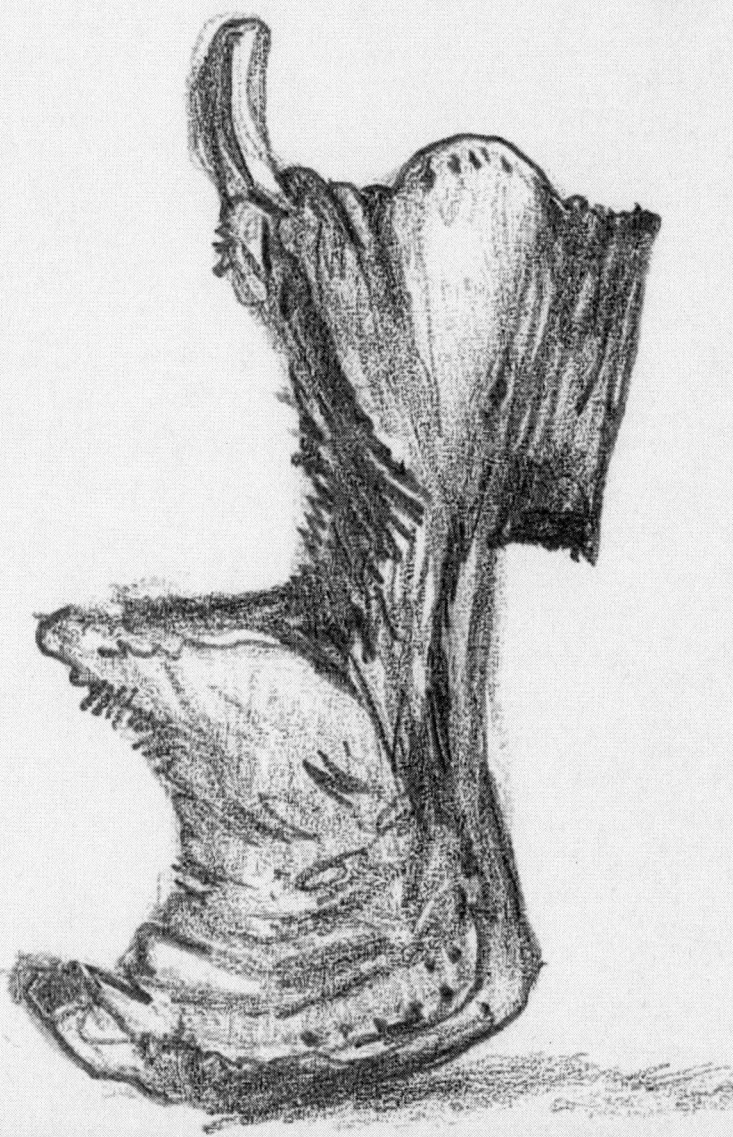

They must all have reached the school at about the same time. It wasn't as if the people who started out first stayed ahead all the way. Some fell behind. Those who were behind began to lead. It was only a half hour walk from the village to the school, but the children took small paths off and back to the main road as they walked, and some, like Koona and Bolu, took to the air to get to school.

Koona didn't remember she had been flying. She was puzzled when other children talked about dreaming. 'What is that?' she would ask. She had never had a dream, or if she had, she didn't remember having had one. If Binu said he had an interesting dream, Koona would say, 'Let me see it too.'

'How can I show you my dream?' Binu would ask.

Bolu explained to Koona that people had to see their dreams by themselves. 'I'm sure you dream. You just forget what you dreamt.'

'I forget nothing,' Koona said. 'Guruji says I have a good memory. All of you get to dream and I never do,' Koona said unhappily.

The cattle were tethered to trees at the edge of the school grounds. A cow had been tethered to a sapling. All the sapling was good for was the rope going slightly taut as the cow pulled. The tautness was sufficient to remind the cow it was tethered. It never pulled harder. The sapling wasn't in danger of being uprooted.

Guruji wanted the old people and children to sleep inside the classrooms, and the young adults to sleep out on the verandah. He suggested bolting the classroom doors from the inside once everyone was settled in, but most doors didn't have a functioning bolt. It was a wonder classroom doors had ever been fitted with bolts on the inside. What purpose did the builders imagine these bolts would serve? Could it be to identify latecomers who would need to wait outside for the door to be opened? Some students came early to prepare the day's lessons. They would go to the watchman's quarters to ask him to let them into a classroom. He would unlock a couple of rooms for them. The classrooms sheltered them from rain and, in the summer, from the heat. In the winter, students liked to prepare for class in the sunlight on the verandah. Many children came early just to play in the school grounds. When the bell rang, everyone hastened to the assembly area for prayer. All the classroom windows opened inside. No one had heard of a classroom window latched on the outside.

There was usually a good reason for a student's being late to school. The students didn't find the school frightening, not even if they had to go there at night. The buzzing in the school sounded like a tree on which hundreds of patrangi birds were alighting for the night.

Chhotu was out of breath when he reached the school. He couldn't tell who was who in all the coming and going. He noticed Bolu sitting in a cubbyhole with his hand on the topmost peg. Bolu seemed lost in thought.

'Bolu!' Chhotu shouted. 'Bolu!'

No response.

'Bolu!' Chhotu decided to try Bolu's voice. First, Bolu was lost in thought. Next, he wouldn't recognize his own voice calling him. The only times he might have heard his name in his own voice would be when he was introducing himself to someone or when he was talking to himself.

Chhotu called out in Premu's voice, then Koona's, then Guruji's. The noise died down when Guruji's voice was heard. Bolu came to himself. He turned towards Guruji's voice and saw Chhotu. Chhotu called him over in Premu's voice. Dropping into Bolu's voice again, he whispered in Bolu's ear, 'Bhaira has fallen into the muram pit and can't climb out.' He whispered the same piece of news in the ear of each of his friends, speaking to them in their own voices.

Because of all the commotion, the friends were able to leave the school without being observed. They were speeding to the pit; they hadn't thought of asking permission to leave the school. Clouds covered the moon as the friends crossed the school grounds. They looked like blobs of fog. People at the school may not have noticed their departure, but the moon kept track of them. It emerged from behind clouds when they left the school and stayed with them, lighting their way, stopping where they stopped. Koona ran to keep up with the group. 'If only we had brought the pony along!' she said.

Bolu walked at the head of the group. He made up a hurry-along song:

> Hurry, scurry, run along.
> Keep pace with the running song.
> Run together, reach together,
> Each of us helping the other.
> We will get there in a trice.
> Running, flying, we'll arrive.

Bolu was growing lighter and lighter. He was unaware that he had left the earth and begun to fly. His friends, too, thought he was running. A wind from the back favoured them all and helped them hurry.

The snack-maker from Bajrang Snack Shop ran as fast as his legs could carry him. He knew he had to get there soon, but he forgot where he was going. He ran past the muram pit before he remembered and trudged back. He thought he heard someone walking behind him, stepping cautiously to avoid making a sound. The snack-maker, too, began stepping cautiously, trying to minimize the crunching of leaves underfoot. He wanted to hear who or what it was that followed him. When the snack-maker took a step, the thing behind took a step. When he stopped, the thing behind stopped. It grew darker.

How was the snack-maker to know that Bolu and his friends had left the school and the moon was guiding them to the muram pit? The snack-maker took his hard plastic shoes off and began to step with utmost care. He heard two people behind him or else a creature with four legs. He prayed it was not a tiger.

The snack-maker's feet were bare. He could feel the scrape of dry leaves. Whatever was behind him was closer now, almost noiseless on what must be padded feet. The snack-maker dared not turn around. He believed that if he looked back he would see a tiger.

If he kept on looking ahead, the creature behind him would not be a tiger.

The snack-maker had been working at the Bajrang Snack Shop for five years. Lately, he had begun to feel afraid for some reason, and wanted to run away. He left work with that intention one day and hid in the jungle. 'I am safe from Bajrang Maharaj,' he thought. Just then he had heard Bajrang Maharaj's voice: 'Be back before it gets dark.' Tigers began to roar in response. A jackal heard the roaring and ran. The snack-maker couldn't remember the way back to the snack shop. He decided to follow the path the jackal took to safety. The jackal ran under a rock behind the pygmy mountain. The snack-maker saw there were two caves under the rock. He wasn't sure which one the jackal had entered. He ran into the one on the right. It was dim inside. He felt his way forward. He recalled that Bajrang Maharaj wanted him back before it got dark. It wasn't that dark yet. There was more and more light as he went forward. Soon he found himself at an opening between two rock walls. A stone lay across the opening like a roof. A narrow path led outside. When he emerged he was surprised to find himself standing before the Bajrang Snack Shop.

A jackal looked down from a rock above him. It must have been commanded to guide him. Was it Bajrang Maharaj who had issued the command?

He bowed his head low, entered the kitchen, and busied himself at his tasks. He kept his head low for days. He would enter the village with his head bowed low, and leave with his head bowed low. He kept his head low when he went to sleep, though it is hard to discern such things in a sleeping form. He felt he could sleep peacefully only with his head bowed low.

He liked unbroken sleep; he was terrified of waking up in the middle of the night. Bajrang Maharaj had told Bhaira to show the snack-maker where to sleep. Bhaira pointed out a corner of the open verandah as the snack-maker's sleeping 'quarters'.

The snack-maker remembered later that the scrunching of leaves in the forest sounded just like the tread of Bajrang Maharaj's country shoes.

His sleep was disturbed one night. He woke up hearing the scrunch of Bajrang Maharaj's country shoes. The sound got fainter, then disappeared. After a while he heard the scrunch of country shoes again. Bajrang Maharaj seemed to have returned to the snack shop and settled down on his chauki. Then it fell quiet, so quiet that the shoes, too, must have fallen asleep. Could it be that Bajrang Maharaj took his after-dinner stroll out in the forest but the scrunch of his shoes sounded like it came from the next room? Could it be that Bajrang Maharaj took his stroll in the forest and the scrunch of his shoes could be heard in the shop? Or could it be that he took his stroll in the shop but the scrunch of his shoes could be heard in the forest? Or could it be that Bajrang Maharaj strolled in the shop while the tiger paced in the forest at the same time, and sounds from shop and forest were simultaneous?

Another day, the snack-maker noticed a large black country shoe by the entrance to the shop.

Where did the shoe come from? Where was its partner? The shoe looked old and wrinkled—too old to have belonged to Bajrang Maharaj. Was it an heirloom handed down from Bajrang Maharaj's father? The sole was studded with hobnails. A tiger could be killed with one blow from this shoe. Not that anyone thought this or said this about the shoe.

Bajrang Maharaj had never been known to come out to the verandah. Could the shoe have walked over to the snack shop entrance on its own? Where would its partner have travelled to? Perhaps Bajrang Maharaj kept the shoe as a pet. 'Here, shoey! Here, shoey!' he would call, and the shoe would come with its tail wagging. The shoe had a tapered leather fold over the end, for convenience in carrying it around or hanging it on a nail in the wall. Shoe-sellers threaded shoes through the leather fold and went from door to door, many pairs of shoes dangling over their shoulders in front and back.

The snack-maker got busy; there were customers at the snack shop. One of the customers saw a shoe travelling across the threshold by itself. He heard the call 'Here, shoey! here shoey!' coming from within the room. The customer had just poured his tea in the saucer to cool it. He was ready to take a cautious first sip. The progress of the shoe across the verandah so amazed him that he drank his tea in the first sip. He didn't even know he had finished the tea. It would have been appropriate to say he had drunk his tea in one breath. Unfortunately, he had trouble taking the next breath. If his breathing hadn't stopped momentarily, it would have been correct to say he was exhaling tea. Be that as it may, he mastered his dread, and left the shop, incredulous that he had seen what he had seen. People wouldn't believe him if he told them.

Thereafter, he was doubly alert when he came in for tea. He would inspect the shoes by the verandah for signs of impulsiveness. Some customers placed their shoes below the verandah before washing hands and feet by the rock. They didn't want to slip wet feet in their shoes for the small distance to the verandah.

One day, a customer couldn't find his shoes. He imagined someone may have put on his shoes in error and left the shop. The earlier customer, who had seen the self-propelled shoe, observed what was going on. 'Are your shoes missing?' he asked the new customer.

'Yes,' the customer replied irritably.

'How can they get lost all by themselves?' the earlier customer asked, feigning amazement.

'Why would they get lost by themselves? I'm the one who lost track of them.' The new customer couldn't understand the question posed to him. 'What do you suggest I do?'

'You shouldn't have taken them off. When you have them on, shoes go where you go. Once you take them off, you are at their mercy. They have minds of their own. Your shoes must have walked off to some destination they favoured. How old were your shoes, did you say? Did you have time to tame them?'

'They were new.'

'That's why. You mustn't have had a chance to break them in. What are you thinking of doing now?'

'I'll have to buy another pair. But I won't repeat my mistake. Either I'll keep them on or stick them in my bag and pull the drawstring tight.' The new customer set off in his bare feet, imagining as he walked that his shoes would turn up somehow. He thought they would meet him on his way home, first the right foot whose sole was a little worn, then the left foot. The left foot would be partly hidden by the side of the road. The right and left foot would both apologize, saying: 'So sorry we had to leave. We didn't know we would be away this long. Please forgive us and put us on again.'

12

In the meantime, Bhaira had begun thinking about a handhold and foothold in the pit. He estimated where he would place his hand and foot, and picked out a sharp-pointed stone from the pile nearby. He started scooping out dirt close to the muram steps with the idea that once he heaved himself up he could use the intact steps to climb out. Then it occurred him that he could gather stones into a new pile and reach the intact steps from the top of the pile. How clever he was! He heaped stones to make a new pile and levelled the top to make a platform. He dug out a handhold. The steps in the muram wall were to his left. He stood on the pile, a hand resting in the handhold, and leapt to the intact step above. The step collapsed while he steadied himself. But he was already on the next step by then. As he stepped out of the pit, he heard the steps he had just climbed on sliding and crashing below.

He was a bird let out of a cage. A newly freed bird wants to fly in any direction available, east or west. The farther it flies the more it believes in its freedom. Freedom means freedom only if it is total. A little freedom means nothing. It's like going from a small cage to a larger cage. Full freedom is no less than the entire sky. Bhaira was free in the entire world, but his immediate goal was the school. He glanced at the sky as he hurried to the school.

The moon, too, had been freed from the pit. It had returned to the unlimited sky, and hurried to the school along with Bhaira. Meanwhile, a moon moved with Bolu and Koona and their friends in the opposite direction, hurrying with them to find Bhaira. It was the same moon, and it shone more radiantly as all the friends came together.

Bhaira was thrilled to see his friends. They turned back towards the school.

The happiness did not last. 'What happened to my bedroll?' Bhaira asked. He stopped and all his friends stopped.

'We can pull it out in the morning,' Chhotu said in Bhaira's voice.

'No. Let's get it out now,' Bhaira spoke in his own voice.

'Tomorrow happens to be a vacation day,' Chhotu said in Bolu's voice.

'Is there something wrong with pulling the bedroll out on a vacation day?' Koona asked.

'It's easy to get the bedroll out on a vacation day. There's a problem only on school days,' Premu said. He was in favour of retrieving the bedroll right then.

'Let's get his bedroll now. It will give him a good night's rest,' Koona said.

The watchman rang the school gong ten times.

'How late it is,' Bolu said, advancing a few paces towards the pit.

Koona lifted her hand to the moon. 'Hold on to my finger,' she said to the moon. 'Don't go wandering off.' Bolu was mumbling to himself and walking ahead. Koona followed behind.

The moon's light or an electric bulb suffices to indicate it's night. To tell day there's only daylight.

The moon let go of Koona's finger. It went behind clouds.

Koona lowered her hand. She reprimanded the moon. 'Now you've gone and fallen into the pit. You need to be more careful.'

The cloud was a piece of darkness the moon should have been careful to avoid.

They arrived at the pit. Bhaira peered in and reported that the bedroll was gone. Someone else must have found it first.

The others looked into the pit. No bedroll.

Bhaira was trying to figure out what to do next when Chhotu spoke in Bhaira's voice: 'What shall we do now?'

Bhaira stayed quiet.

Chhotu said in Bhaira's voice: 'I'll get yelled at by Bajrang Maharaj.'

Everyone moved closer to Bhaira. He nodded his head. 'That's true,' he said.

'Who could have made away with the bedroll?' Bhaira wondered.

Chhotu spoke in Bhaira's voice: 'The snack-maker must have picked up the bedroll.'

'In that case, there's nothing to worry about,' Bhaira's friends said.

They all turned back towards the school.

The children at the school had kept a lookout for Bolu and his friends; they wanted to play together before going to sleep. Some mumbling could be heard from where the children lay, but they were more asleep than awake. One of them might wake up and ask a question, and fall back to sleep before receiving an answer. Two friends might be talking. One of them would drift into sleep and the other fall asleep at the same time. A child might say, 'Bolu must be on his way here. Let me go out and see,' and roll over on his side, already asleep. The other child might say, 'If he's back, he must be sleeping. If he's not back, I'll stay awake and let you know when he gets here.' Then the other child would also drop off to sleep.

The first child would sit up. 'Let's go find Bolu,' he would say and fall asleep sitting up.

The other child would awaken and see his friend sitting up, 'Why did you go to see Bolu without telling me?' He would shake his friend. 'Why didn't you tell me?'

The first child would open his eyes, 'I told you Bolu must be awake. He must be getting things ready for tomorrow. Let me sleep.' He would fall back asleep sitting up.

Eventually everyone fell asleep. The snores of the elders made the silence audible.

Bolu and his friends walked noisily. They neared the Bajrang Snack Shop on their way to the school. Premu thought he heard a growl coming from the shop. 'There's a tiger in there,' Premu exclaimed. Bhaira paid no attention.

'It sounds like a tiger,' Koona said, and ran to where Bolu walked ahead.

She slipped her hand in his. A low growling continued intermittently, as if the tiger had felled its prey and was resting before dinner. The others were alarmed at the sounds, but Bolu and Bhaira showed no fear.

Whom could the tiger have preyed on at the snack shop? Knocking Bajrang Maharaj down was out of the question. Nor could the tiger have gotten in past Bajrang Maharaj's wary eye. It must be that Bajrang Maharaj had gone out and the tiger had attacked the snack-maker.

'The tiger must have known Bajrang Maharaj was out,' Bolu said loudly, walking ahead once more. The others quickened their pace to catch up. Bolu hopped forward with each word he uttered: 'The–

tiger-must-have-attacked-the-snack!' He laughed and took hold of Bhaira's hand, half-dragging him as they walked together. 'First the tiger captures its prey, then it makes a meal of the prey.'

'It must have been hiding behind a rock near the stove. The tiger would have entered just as the snack-maker tilted the hot snacks into the serving dish. The customers would have fled in fear. The tiger would have pounced on the snacks. When it lifted its paw there would be pieces of potato dipped in batter in each claw. The tiger would raise the paw to its mouth.' It was like a customer eating snacks with a fork.

'Listen, Bhaira,' Bolu said, 'and don't pretend you can't hear. Can you still make out growling sounds from the shop?' He took hold of Bhaira's hand again.

'I don't hear any sounds,' Bhaira declared.

'Then what do you hear?' the others asked him. They stopped walking and stood around Bhaira. Bolu had released his hold on Bhaira. He stood a few paces away from the group.

Bhaira moved towards Bolu. 'The sound is my father snoring.'

'Could it be a tiger snoring?' Koona asked anxiously.

'What's there to fear if the tiger is asleep?' Binu spoke in a whisper so as not to wake the tiger.

'Don't be afraid. It's just my father snoring.' Bhaira whispered as well, not out of fear the tiger would wake up, but out of fear his father would.

'It's not morning yet,' Bolu said.

His friends nodded agreement. 'It's not morning yet.'

Bolu began to sing:

> We'll look for Morning
> In the forest
> On vacation day.
> Wake up, wake up Bajrang Maharaj
> And ask him please to say
> 'Tea and snacks for Morning!'
> Keep Morning busy at play.
> We won't let Morning leave us
> Find it a place to stay
> We'll follow the new rule
> Enroll it in our school.

The friends resumed their walk to school. Through his nostrils widened from snoring, Bajrang Maharaj was able to smell Bhaira's presence. The snoring ceased. The children were startled by the cessation of noise. 'BHAIRA!' Bajrang Maharaj called out. This 'BHAIRA!' even the deaf would have heard. 'Have you come for your bedroll? It's on the table in the verandah.' There was an answering roar from the forest. Then the growling resumed.

'He must have gone to sleep,' the friends thought.

'Yes, my father is snoring now,' Bhaira said.

'You might as well pick up your bedroll,' Bolu suggested, walking towards the snack shop as he spoke.

The snoring sounded louder with each step they took towards the shop. They walked cautiously, pausing at the base of the verandah. Bhaira climbed up alone. It was dark but Bhaira could make out something on the table folded in extra layers of darkness. He slipped it under his arm.

'Are you leaving?' Bajrang Maharaj asked.

Bhaira hurried down the steps. He knew that his father could wake up in an instant if that is what he wanted to do.

Their walk was more like running. Koona noticed the moon stealing a look from behind a cloud.

'There's no tiger in there,' she said.

The moon came out reassured.

'You were afraid, weren't you?' Koona said to the moon.

Bolu walked ahead humming to himself.

Everyone was asleep at the school. Bolu's mother had made room for him before she fell asleep. He went and lay next to her.

Koona's mother slept nearby. She, too, had made room for her child. Koona curled in there and fell asleep instantly.

She had a dream. It may have been her first dream. She may have seen dreams earlier and forgotten them by morning. This, too, may be a dream she would forget and claim she never dreamt, and ask her friends to please teach her how to dream, or at least how to view their dreams.

She saw that Bolu called her by name but she pretended not to hear. Then she saw a girl, who looked like Koona when she saw herself in the mirror, walking towards Bolu in response to his call. The girl walked towards Bolu, just as Koona walked when she saw herself walking in a mirror. The girl went and stood next to Bolu, who was also visible in the mirror. While Koona slept, she saw the mirror Koona atop the pygmy mountain. There was Bolu there, and Premu, Bhaira and Binu. She asked the mirror Koona if she knew where Chhotu might be. The mirror Koona ignored the question and walked over to the mouth of the hole where all her friends were.

'Let's make a rope of us strung together,' the mirror Koona said, 'and get down to the bottom using ourselves. Bhaira weighs the most among us. He'll lie down by the hole and support us as we go down. The first person on the rope will be the one who is lightest.'

Koona could see that Bolu took hold of mirror Koona's hand. Bolu lay down at the mouth of the hole and mirror Koona dangled in the hole. Chhotu kept a good hold on Bolu's feet. Bolu let Koona's weight pull him towards the hole while Koona dangled down another few inches. Chhotu lay down next, maintaining his grip on Bolu's feet. Binu took hold of Chhotu's feet while Chhotu slipped into the hole. Premu took hold of Binu's feet. Bhaira took hold of Premu's feet.

'You can edge into the hole now,' Bhaira said to Premu. Bhaira lay belly down at the mouth of the hole, balancing the weight of the human rope.

Koona said nothing while she hung suspended the deepest in the hole. It was hard to guess what she could view.

'Can you see anything?' Bolu asked her.

Koona was the only one with her head up. The others were hanging upside down.

Bolu's feet moved as if he was walking. Chhotu spoke to Bolu in Bhaira's voice: 'Don't say anything. Otherwise, we won't be able to hold on to your feet.' The entire rope had trembled when Bolu spoke to Koona. Koona saved herself from hitting the wall. 'I can see a beehive,' she said with effort. 'Please don't speak, Bolu. I don't want to knock against the hive.'

Chhotu heard what she said. He repeated in Koona's voice, 'I can see a beehive.' The ones above Chhotu thought they heard Koona speaking directly. Bhaira didn't pretend not to hear. He paid full attention.

'There are no bees in the beehive,' Koona added.

Chhotu repeated the message in Koona's voice.

The message pleased Bhaira. He crept forward a little. He wanted to see the beehive for himself.

Bolu could see the beehive, but said nothing.

Chhotu's arms were hurting from carrying the weight of Bolu and Koona. He didn't know in whose voice he should say that his arms were hurting so his friends knew he was talking about himself. 'I am Chhotu,' he said to Binu. 'I am speaking in Bolu's voice. My arms are hurting. I won't be able to bear the weight of Bolu and Koona much longer. Please ask Premu to pull us up.'

Binu's arms were also hurting. 'Please ask Bhaira to pull us up,' he said to Premu. 'Our arms are hurting.'

'I'll pull us up,' Bhaira said when Premu relayed Binu's message.

The ground was uneven behind where Bhaira lay. It was hard for him to snake backwards against the weight of the others. 'It's hard to manage,' he said to Premu.

Premu relayed the message to Binu, Binu to Chhotu, Chhotu, between sobs, to Bolu. 'Don't say anything about this, Bolu.'

Small stones dug into Bhaira's arms. Premu's nose got skinned as he crawled out. He was holding Binu's feet with all his might. Bhaira helped Premu pull Binu up. They all came out of the hole except Koona, who still wanted to discover what lay below. She let go of Bolu's hand, but Bolu held on to her. She awoke just then, leaving the dream behind in her sleep. She retained no memory of the dream.

The children in the school had been dreaming. 'We saw dreams!' they shouted. 'I've never seen one,' Koona said. 'Let me see your dream. Please.'

The vacation day had begun. People woke up late; they must have been caught up in morning dreams. Bolu remembered what he dreamt. He dreamt he was walking silently. The sound of his own voice reached him from far away.

When Bolu narrated his dream, Chhotu said it must have been him speaking in Bolu's voice. 'Bolu was able to walk without speaking because I supplied his voice,' Chhotu said in Bolu's voice.

But Bolu didn't start walking. He stood there yawning.

'You were talking so loudly in your dream, Bolu could hear it in his,' Premu said.

'I slept next to Chhotu. Why couldn't I hear him in my dream?' Binu wondered.

'You were some distance from where Bolu slept. Chhotu was talking in Bolu's voice. If Chhotu had been speaking in his own voice you would have heard him,' Premu replied.

'Let's wake Bhaira up,' Bolu said, walking towards where Bhaira lay sleeping.

'It won't be easy for him to get up. He's tired,' Koona said.

'Why is he tired?' Bolu wondered.

The friends walked along with Bolu and

Koona, listening to their conversation. The school grounds had emptied of mothers, grandfathers, grandmothers, uncles, cows and calves. Koona's pony wasn't there either.

All these guests left when it was morning. They had made the school feel like home.

Now it was school again. The teachers got busy with their tasks. A teacher was heading to an empty classroom. He thought Koona wanted to ask him something and stopped for her, but she didn't say anything. 'Nice dreams come true,' he said to her. He was gone from the verandah before she could tell him she had never had a dream.

The children woke up late even though they had wanted to wake up early. In the meantime, the previous night had been added to their vacation day, including its morning dreams. Dreaming was indeed a kind of experience. In dreams, a non-swimmer could experience swimming across the sea. Awake, the non-swimmer would drown in a ditch.

Everyone was talking at the same time. Bolu would stop while he listened, walk while he spoke. The others walked and stopped as he did. Their random movement and their colourful clothes made them look like a centipede with bright markings.

Koona wore a red skirt and an orange top. Bolu wore brown shorts and a dark maroon shirt, his skin colour blending with the colour of his clothes.

Premu wore khaki shorts and a printed shirt. Binu wore white cotton pajamas and a maroon shirt darker than Bolu's. Chhotu's shorts were a dark navy, easily mistaken for black. His shirt was iridescent, one colour in the sun, another in the shade—indefinite like his voice. The indefiniteness might extend over time to his appearance as well. His appearance might change as he grew older. At first he would appear to be Chhotu. Then he would appear to be like Chhotu. Then he would become quite different. He would come to meet his friends and say, 'I'm Chhotu.' His friends would recognize him because he spoke in Koona's voice. What if he used a voice unfamiliar to his friends?

Bhaira slumbered, arms crossed over the chest, cap in his hands. He held on to the cap even in sleep.

When he had lain down to sleep, he was thinking about how he had told his father everyone was expected to be present for vacation day school. Mothers and fathers were expected to be present. Grandmothers, grandfathers, lions, tigers, wolves, and bears were expected to be present. He hadn't planned on mentioning forest animals. He hoped his father would come, but without bringing along the animals Bhaira had spoken of inadvertently. He had looked around before he fell asleep; his father hadn't arrived.

Bhaira lay with his eyes shut, seeing images in his mind. Then he dropped into real dreaming.

He saw that the others were sleeping; he was the only one awake. The moon was sometimes bright, sometimes dark. His friends had abandoned him. He was looking for his father. Students were asleep in each of the classrooms. The moon vanished behind clouds as soon as he came out to the verandah. The bulb went out. As suddenly as it had turned dark, it grew light again. The moon escaped from clouds. The bulb came on. The moon disappeared behind clouds. The bulb went out. How can moon and light bulb work simultaneously? Bhaira wondered.

He felt for the switch in the dark and flipped it on. The moon shone again, clear of clouds. In a little while, moon and bulb went dark again. He felt for the switch. He was pleased to find it in the off position; he had discovered a new magic trick. It stayed dark in the sky.

He heard voices, but couldn't see who was approaching. Why is the moon hiding? he thought to himself. He stepped towards the edge of the verandah to see better. He couldn't make anything out. He went back to the wall and felt for the switch.

He flipped it on. The moon flashed in the sky like a hundred-watt bulb. The bulb in the verandah, too, came on, brighter than before, as if from a surge in voltage.

He saw his father entering the school grounds accompanied by a lion, a tiger, a wolf and a bear. Sometimes the bear walked on four legs, sometimes on two. It walked more slowly when standing on its hind legs. At full height it was taller than his father. The bear walked on all fours until it was abreast of his father. Then it walked on two legs. They continued walking together, his father's left hand resting on the bear's back. Bhaira could see white lines in the shape of the letter V within the dark hair on the bear's chest. He seemed to be seeing through a zoom lens. Along with the animals, he could see tiny insects against the light of the moon. But for some reason, the zoom lens would not focus on his father; he looked hazy. Could it be that his father carried the semi-darkness of the Bajrang Snack Shop with him? That, added to the darkness outside, might account for the haziness. People carry some essential things with them when they leave home: glasses, umbrella, cloth bag, handkerchief, cap. His father must have taken darkness along. Never in his life had Bhaira succeeded in getting a clear view of his father.

Bhaira slumbered. Bolu walked around him in a

circle, saying, 'Bhaira, wake up. Bhaira, wake up.' Koona tried to shake him awake. The friends shouted, 'Up, Bhaira!' to no avail.

'He won't wake up,' Binu said. 'Remember how he slept through lessons?'

Chhotu spoke in Guruji's voice, 'He's alone, trapped in a bad dream. We must help him.'

'How can we help him?' Koona asked, yawning.

'He'll get out of the dream if we get him out of sleeping,' Binu said. He took hold of Bhaira's arm and pulled so Bhaira would sit up. The others helped Binu pull. They could get Bhaira to sit, even though his eyes were shut. As soon as they released his arm, he rolled back down. He began to snore, making a moaning sound as he exhaled. It must have been from the bad dream.

'How can we help him inside his dream?' Koona asked, yawning still.

'I'll get some water to splash on his face,' Chhotu said in the watchman's voice, and ran to fetch some. Koona lay down on a rug nearby. She fell asleep, and joined Bhaira in his dream. In the dream, Koona went and stood by Bhaira. She saw a lion, a tiger, a wolf and a bear accompany Bajrang Maharaj to the school grounds. She felt afraid.

'Now's a fine time to arrive,' Bhaira said. 'Were all of you asleep?'

'We were awake,' Koona said. 'We were trying

hard to wake you up. I fell asleep again so I could help you. You didn't wake up.'

'But I am awake,' Bhaira said. 'And you're awake.' He didn't know he was dreaming.

In her dream Koona remembered she had been awake. She wanted to tell Bolu and the others that they should go to sleep and enter Bhaira's dream. She called out to them but no one heard her.

Bolu saw her sleeping and tried to wake her. 'Get up,' he said to Koona, and took two or three steps back. 'Get up,' he said again, and took two or three steps towards her. He decided to sit down next to her. The others sat around them.

'What should we do?' the others said.

They saw Bolu yawning.

'It's vacation day. We don't need to do anything,' Chhotu said in Bolu's voice.

They turned to Bolu on hearing his voice and saw he was asleep. They, too, lay down and slept. Soon they were seeing the same dream as Bhaira and Koona. Koona clapped with joy at seeing Bolu in the dream. Bhaira stopped feeling anxious. Together the friends began thinking about what they needed to do.

There were swarms of insects around the bulb in the school. The moon was a spotlight tracking the villagers. Insects swayed and reeled in that column of light. They were in danger of smashing against the moon. Some insects were already trapped in the bear's coat of dark fur.

'We are coming,' Bajrang Maharaj rumbled as clouds rumble. The lion and the tiger roared. The wolf howled. Lightning flashed with a crackling sound. The moon hid behind clouds. The bulb went out. Darkness engulfed the school.

'The bulb is out. The moon is gone,' Bolu said, bumping into Bhaira as he spoke. Bhaira stumbled and hit the wall. He would have fallen if the wall hadn't stopped him.

'Must have been Bolu,' Bhaira said.

'Don't say anything while it's dark,' Koona said.

'Stay where you are,' Binu added.

'Turn on the light,' Bhaira said while feeling for the switch along the wall. Koona wasn't feeling for the switch. She knew her hand wouldn't reach that high.

'There's no power,' Bolu said. He had reached the alcove next to the switch.

Bhaira had bumped into Bolu and lost his bearings momentarily; he couldn't figure out where the switch should be.

'Don't say anything,' Bhaira told Bolu. 'Otherwise you'll knock against me again.'

'I won't speak a word,' Bolu said, climbing up to the alcove. There was a flutter of wings. He had startled some pigeons.

'Feel for the switch where you are. The moon will come out when you flip it on.'

Bolu had estimated correctly. The switch was within reach of the alcove. He flipped it, and moon and bulb came on.

The friends looked beyond the verandah. There was no sign of Bajrang Maharaj, Bear, Lion, Tiger or Wolf. Where could they have gone? A light rain began to fall. The night's blue mixed with the moonlight. The shower beyond the verandah appeared composed not of water but of light.

'Let's play in the rain,' Bolu said. He had stepped outside before the others could hold him back. A shimmering rain soaked his clothes. A hole in the clouds made the moon shine upon him like a pillar of light. A pigeon flew out of a classroom transom and hovered over him. Then it began to climb towards the moon. Bolu raised his right arm and followed the pigeon, keeping within the pillar of light.

'Don't go away, Bolu!' the others pleaded.

Bolu had his gaze fixed on the moon. The pillar of light began to contract and draw back towards the moon, as if it had been a net to catch Bolu in. Could Bajrang Maharaj, Bear, Lion, Tiger and Wolf been hauled up in the moon's net as Bolu had been, or would they be lurking somewhere around the school? They may have found a safe corner for themselves. It was true that no one had a clear impression of Bajrang Maharaj's countenance in any case. His features were indistinct at a distance. They grew even more indistinct as he drew nearer. When he was very close he seemed to disappear. Was the defect something a good pair of reading glasses could correct?

The dream was now a sea on which the friends navigated a bamboo raft.

There was no land in sight. They used a bamboo pole to push against the bottom and propel the raft forward. The waves were high. A large moon rode in the sky as before. The raft would rise close to the moon as the waves surged. Koona could make out Bolu's form on the moon. 'I can see Bolu,' Koona said. He seemed to be talking to himself as he walked. They waited for a wave to raise them so they could call out to Bolu, 'Jump on the raft, Bolu!', but the wave subsided before Bolu could leap. They decided they would be the ones to leap the next time. They would leap onto the moon. Koona was ready. A wave rose. She leapt upon the moon. At the same time Bolu jumped towards the raft. Bhaira, Binu, Premu and Chhotu saw that neither Koona nor Bolu succeeded in their aim. Meanwhile, the surge abated. The sea grew calm like water in a pond.

The friends were horrified. They huddled together, eyes filled with tears, trying in vain to comfort one another.

What happened was that when Bolu jumped, he fell on the grass-top roof. And when Koona leapt, she fell on the grass-top roof. They landed near one another.

'Is this what grass on the moon is like?' Koona asked.

'We are on the grass-top roof on earth,' Bolu responded.

'But I leapt towards the moon.'

'You missed your aim. The moon rises by the grass-top roof.'

The two walked together on the roof.

'Who is that?' an ancient-sounding voice asked from below. 'Is it a cat? If it's a cat let it say meow.'

'They'll get angry if I say I am Koona,' she thought. She lied: 'Meow!' and instantly turned into a cat.

Bolu was frightened by the change in Koona. He picked her up. 'This is Bolu speaking,' he said. He had been standing near the edge of the roof. He fell off the roof as he spoke, and landed before the very old man and the very old woman. They were seated outside their door with a water jug between them. They were brushing their teeth with datun twigs.

'Is it morning already?' Bolu said as he walked towards them.

'Ours, yes,' they said, 'yours, not yet. Our morning begins just past midnight. We wake up then and begin to brush our teeth. We keep brushing our teeth till the entire datun twig is used up.'

Bolu glanced down and saw that ten feet of datun twig trailed along the ground. The cat was restless. Bolu wondered what it would take to turn it into Koona again.

'Were you the one who jumped onto the roof,' the very old woman asked, 'or was it the cat?'

'We both jumped,' Bolu answered. 'I wanted to jump to where Koona was on the raft. She wanted to jump to where I was on the moon. We both missed our aim and landed on your roof.'

'Is it your cat?'

'We go to the same school.'

'Does the cat study at the school with you, or does it live in your textbook?' the very old man asked with a smile. His teeth were gleaming white.

'There is a cat in my textbook. This one isn't even in my class. She's in a different class.'

Bolu remembered the very old man had taken him in his lap once and stroked his head. He remembered the very old man had no teeth.

'But you have teeth,' Bolu said. Bolu would walk ahead when he spoke and walk back when he spoke again. 'I saw you once before and at that time you didn't have any teeth.'

'That must have been my older brother. He's the

toothless one. He's a hundred and fifty years older than me and needs a walking stick to get about.'

The very old woman interrupted, 'Not a hundred and fifty years older. A hundred and seventy-six years older.'

'Is he home just now?' Bolu asked as he walked towards her.

'He's gone for his walk.'

'This late at night?' Bolu said and drew closer.

The cat jumped from his lap into the very old woman's lap. The very old woman began stroking it with her left hand while she continued brushing her teeth with her right. 'Day and night mean nothing to him. He takes a stroll from the past to the future whenever he wishes, and returns home whenever he wishes. I hear the tapping of his walking stick. He will cross in front of the hut soon, travelling from the past to the present, and from there, just beyond us, into the future.' She gestured with the hand holding the datun twig.

'Can I travel to the future?'

'Isn't that where you are going now, growing taller and more mature every day?'

Bolu saw that Koona had returned to her original form while she sat in the very old woman's lap. 'You're Koona again!' Bolu exclaimed.

'The cat was a lie,' the very old woman commented. 'The truth is Koona. A lie can last a little while. The truth lasts forever.' Her teeth shone when she laughed. Though the very old couple's hair had turned white they did not need the support of walking sticks.

Koona was smiling.

'Don't you want to go home?' Bolu asked.

'I can hear the tap tap of his stick. Elder Brother is approaching us,' the very old man said.

The very old woman set Koona down. Both the very old woman and the very old man rose to greet their elder relative. The very old woman covered her head with the end of the sari in the traditional way of showing respect. The very old man saw that his elder brother rested his hand on his sister-in-law's shoulder for support.

Koona said namaste. The couple blessed her. Bolu bowed down and touched their feet.

'You forgot your walking stick, Brother,' the very old man said.

'I had your sister-in-law for support.'

'I heard tapping sounds and thought it was your walking stick.'

'You mistook my wooden sandals for the walking stick.'

'Would you like me to fetch the walking stick for you?' the very old man asked.

'Not needed,' Elder Brother said. 'Your sister-in-law is fine support.'

'Do you hear how Brother-in-law is saying nice things about you?' the very old man said to his sister-in-law.

His sister-in-law smiled. 'I'm not hard of hearing,' she said.

The very old woman was pleased by the banter. She smiled, too.

Elder Brother walked into the future with his hand on his wife's shoulder and wooden sandals on his feet.

The pigeon that had climbed ahead of Bolu along the pillar of light was still with him. It had flown to be near him when Bolu jumped from the moon. When Koona turned into a cat, the pigeon had found safety in a nearby peepal tree.

The others on the raft were baffled. Where could Koona and Bolu be? Was it safe where they were? The turbulence subsided. The water grew calm, but the water level continued to drop as if the sea was emptying. The water level dropped till it merged with the bottom. Then the land, upon which their raft rested, began to sink. 'Everyone lean their weight on our pole,' Binu said. 'If we stake our pole deep, we might keep the earth from sinking.' They exerted their weight. The pole went in straight. The sinking slowed, then stopped. The friends found themselves dangling at one end of the pole.

Bolu and Koona stood on the earth before them.

Koona was calling them by name. Chhotu was the lowest on the pole. He climbed down carefully till he reached Bolu and Koona below. The others got down by turns.

Bhaira was not among them.

It turned out the snack-maker had succeeded in waking Bhaira. Bhaira had woken Premu. Premu had woken the others. Koona alone remained in the dream, sobbing audibly. The others woke her from her sleep. Her cheeks were wet.

'Were you dreaming?' they asked in one voice. Bolu's voice was among those asking. His feet dangled from the alcove.

The sun had climbed.

'You've been sleeping late on vacation day,' Guruji said. 'Go wash up. Breakfast will be ready soon.' The school had its own well and hand pump.

'Did you dream?' Binu asked, as Koona rose to go to the well.

'No,' Koona said and continued walking. She didn't say anything to Bolu.

'Where are you going, Koona?' Chhotu asked her in Bolu's voice.

'I have a new name from today. I'm not Koona any longer.'

'What's your new name?' Bolu asked walking towards Koona.

'Sea,' she answered.

'The school register says Koona.' Bolu walked beside her.

'Today is vacation day.'

'Will your name become Koona again tomorrow?'

'No. It will remain "Sea".'

14

Koona went to her teacher. Her teacher was busy preparing breakfast for the assembly. Some children laid out rows of leaf plates along the Long School verandah. Bolu and her friends accompanied Koona.

'You aren't ready, Koona. Everyone needs to have washed their face and combed their hair. You haven't even brushed your teeth!'

'My name isn't Koona.'

'Is that because today is vacation day?' the teacher asked.

'My name won't be Koona on a school day either.'

'In that case, they'll drop you from the school roll,' the teacher said.

'Her name is Sea,' Bhaira said to the teacher.

Koona nodded agreement.

'I want you to tell me yourself. What's your name?'

'Sea. Just like the sea with big waves,' Koona responded.

'What does the name Koona mean?' the teacher asked.

'I don't know,' Koona said.

'All right, Sea. Go take a bath and get ready quickly. The food may be gone by the time you return.'

'Sea, would you take a bath if your name was Well?' Bolu asked.

Koona broke into a dance, beating time with her feet:

> If I was River, I would bathe
> If I was Water, I would bathe
> Soaking in it all day long
> If I was Waterfall I'd drop
> Down from rock to lower rock
> Rub my back against the stone
> Wash with droplets when it rains
> Wash with waves when it pours
> Wash with care when it's dry.

Bolu asked as he danced to the beat:

> How will you bathe when there's drought?

Koona replied:

> I will turn into steam and bathe with vapour.
> I will turn into sea and bathe with foam.

A pulley was mounted on the well. Bhaira told Sea that if she sat in the bucket at one end of the rope, he would give her a quick dip in the water. He would let the bucket down into the well and pull it up again.

'I'm not mad,' she said. 'What if the rope slips

from your hand? I'll die if you keep me under the water too long. I'll tell the teacher about this. Bolu! Where are you?' she called out.

Bhaira ran away.

'What happened?' Bolu asked as he walked towards her.

Then Bolu, Koona, Premu, Binu and Chhotu bathed by the well; Bhaira bathed by the hand pump. He kept a safe distance from Koona; she had told the others that Bhaira wanted her to ride the water bucket for a dip in the well. He wanted to put her in danger.

This episode gave Bolu a new idea. There was still half the vacation day left. What if they brought a pulley to the mouth of the hole in the mountain and climbed down, holding on to one end of the rope? 'Let's eat first,' he said, 'then let's try using a pulley.' He walked up to Bhaira and invited him to join in the scheme.

There was an unused pulley in Bolu's house and no well. He had asked his mother about this a few days earlier. 'We have a pulley,' Bolu said, 'but no well.' She had answered that there were many wells that had no pulleys.

'Why didn't you give the pulley away to someone who could use it?'

'How could I? It isn't ours. It was here before we built our house.'

The pulley was a small size meant for a well with a small mouth. Could it have been designed for descent to the bottom of the mountain?

15

Breakfast consisted of garbanzos boiled in salt water, buttermilk, jaggery, a guava each, sweet puris, squash and plain rice. Everyone wrapped their jaggery in green leaves and packed it away for later. The friends ate quickly and ran to Bolu's house. His mother was not at home. An iron bar and pulley rested against the side of the house. Bhaira hoisted the bar and pulley on his shoulder. Then the friends ran to the pygmy mountain, eager to get there before the grown-ups found out what the children were up to.

They placed the pulley over the mouth of the hole. It fit nicely. The bar lay securely across the hole, with the pulley attached to the center. Bolu walked up and down while the friends sat in the shade of a rock.

'We'll need a long rope,' he said.

'We have a rope for the well at home,' Premu responded.

'It's a deep hole. The well rope will be short.' He walked out of the shadows into the sun. 'We'll need a rope at least seven days long.' He returned to where the friends were.

'How do we measure length in days?' Binu asked.

'We start letting down the rope at dawn and keep

letting down the rope till dusk. A rope that long is one day long,' Bolu replied.

'Does that mean you'll stay out of school seven days?' Chhotu asked in Guruji's voice.

'We'll ask Guruji to excuse us, but first let's find some rope. We still have half our vacation day left. Let's get half-a-day's length of rope. We can try the two rope makers in the village,' Bolu said.

An old man sat outside a hut twisting twine. A heap of finished rope lay by his side.

'We need a long rope, Father,' Koona said, 'seven days long.'

'Since I was ten years old,' the rope maker said, 'I have been twisting this one piece of rope. I am ninety-nine now. The rope is eighty-nine years long. You can cut off a seven-day length if you want. But it may be easier for you to go to my brother. He makes a new rope each day. He might have a seven-day one lying around.'

'Koona, we don't need a seven-day rope, only a half-a-day rope. How will we transport a seven-day rope to the mountain?' Bolu asked as they walked together.

'My name isn't Koona, it's Sea. If we get shorter ropes, we'll have many knots.'

'Half a day is six hours. Let's get two three-hour ropes. That'll require only a single knot,' Bolu said.

He began to sing:

> How many instants to a one-minute string?
> How many parts? How long each part?
> Twine the instants of life together
> Let down the bucket to quench the thirst
> Unslaked thirst for the infinite.
> Let down the bucket into the water,
> Build the strength to haul it up.

They went to the younger brother. He, too, was busy twisting twine. Many coils of rope lay near where he sat. Bolu began talking as he approached, 'Father, we need half-a-day's length of rope.'

'Son, a day from dawn to dusk is the length I make. Each coil is a day's length. I have never worked only half a day. The ropes in the heap are one-day long. I never leave my work unfinished. You are welcome to a take a day-long coil if you like.'

'We only need half-a-day's length, Father. We only have half the vacation day left,' Premu said.

'I even have a rope that is two days and one night long. I don't have just a night-long piece. The nights I can't sleep I keep adding on to the day's work all night. I add the next day's work to the same rope. Tell me what you'd like.'

They couldn't decide.

'We'll ask Guruji for an extra vacation day,' Koona said, and turning to the younger rope maker she asked if they could have the two-days-and-one-night long rope.

The rope maker picked up a coil of rope and handed it to Koona.

Koona placed it on her shoulder.

'This is such a small piece of rope,' Bhaira remarked.

'It's not that small,' Bolu said. 'Maybe it'll grow with time as we do. Meanwhile, the vacation day is passing. Let's get back.'

16

It could be that the inside of the pygmy mountain was the inside of a dormant volcano. It was hard to tell what could have hollowed the mountain out. The elders who visited the mountain said nothing about it. They knew only that there wasn't much mountain left to hollow out. If it was a volcano, it had spent its energy, and could be considered extinct.

What if it turned out, once the friends descended into the mountain's core, that the volcano was still active?

There was a flourishing maulsari tree near the mouth of the hole. They wrapped one end of the rope around the maulsari, wishing the trunk had been less slender. The tree shook as they worked. Small orange berries dropped to the ground. The berries had hard crusts and thin layers of pulp. They tasted like unripe persimmons. The friends picked the fallen berries and stuffed them in their pockets for later.

'We don't have much time,' Koona said while the others were securing the rope. 'Can't Bhaira hold the rope while Bolu and I start going down?' she then asked.

'We'll all go down together,' Bolu replied.

'I want to go first,' Koona insisted.

Chhotu imitated the snack-maker's voice: 'Then you'll be the first to get stung by bees.'

'I know the hive is empty,' Koona said.

'How do you know?' Bolu said, climbing to the top of a rock. 'Did you have a dream about the hive?'

'I wish I knew how to dream. Nobody taught me how.'

'We don't know how to dream either. We just dream. If we knew the method we would teach you,' Bolu said climbing down from the rock.

'Time to descend!' he announced.

'I'll go first,' Koona said. 'I want to hold this end of the rope. I will go down a day and a night and another day.'

The rope had been mounted on the pulley. Koona was the first to hold the rope. She was quiet as she descended. Bolu followed her. Their weight pulled on the rope. It began to let down fast even though the others tried to release it gradually.

'Bhaira!' the snack-maker called out. He had spotted Bhaira and the others as he looked up from the Bajrang Snack Shop. He had also got a good view of Bolu when Bolu climbed up on the rock.

Bhaira turned to see where the voice came from and loosened his grip on the rope. The pulley spun free.

'Grab the rope, Bhaira!' the others shouted.

Bhaira tightened his hold on the rope and stopped the pulley. The rope must have descended many hours.

'We are hours behind Koona and Bolu now,' the others said, except for Bhaira, who kept quiet.

'The snack-maker will be on his way here. Father must be asking for me,' Bhaira said.

Binu poked his head into the hole. 'Koona!' he called out.

She replied from wherever she was: 'My name is Sea.'

'Are the two of you all right?'

'Yes.'

She whispered to Bolu that he should not respond. 'If you speak, you'll wave your legs. We might hit against a rock.'

Koona was able to take advantage of her dream. She had no memory of the dream, but she remembered the experience.

Bolu wanted to say something. He couldn't gesture easily; he was holding on to the rope. He gripped the rope tight with his right hand and signaled with the left. He mumbled, 'Look!' in Koona's ear. A small plant with two leaves could be seen where Bolu pointed. If there was a plant, there must be water. The leaves of the plant were pale yellow.

It was Bolu's mumbling that made the rope sway, but Koona thought the swaying came from two people weighing down a rope.

At the same time, they could feel cool air flowing up from below. Bolu mumbled again. 'The mountain is breathing,' he said, 'and we are inside its belly.'

'Is this really a mountain or a python in the shape of a mountain?'

They heard a rumbling sound. 'The mountain is belching,' Koona said.

'We've been digested in the mountain's belly,' Bolu mumbled. 'The mountain is belching satisfaction.'

'We haven't been digested yet. Otherwise we wouldn't be able to speak,' Koona said.

The rumbling grew louder. 'The dead volcano comes to life!' Bolu said, more loudly than before. The rope swayed wide. They forgot that the swaying was from the movement of Bolu's feet. 'It could be an earthquake, Koona,' Bolu said. 'It sounds like an earthquake. Maybe there'll be an eruption of lava and we will be carried out by lava.'

Koona didn't react to being called Koona. 'If the lava carries us out we will be cinder.'

They looked down to see if there were orange flames below. They needn't have looked. The orange of the lava would spread through the darkness on its own. Rising waves of heat would cause blisters on their skin. The rope they held on to would ignite. Hot air would roast them before they fell into the lava. It was well-known that a customer coming close to the Bajrang oven would suffer thermal burns.

'How are you down there? We've heard nothing from you.' Was that Bhaira himself speaking or Chhotu using Bhaira's voice?

'Is that you, Bhaira?' Koona asked.

The rumbling did not subside.

Bajrang Maharaj's room was a scrapheap of darkness: there were old bits of darkness and there were very old bits of darkness. It was possible that a tunnel led from the cave-like room deep into the mountain.

'Sea! Sea! Sea!' Premu called down.

Koona was unable to hear him over the rumbling of the mountain.

The friends standing above could hear the rumbling as well.

Premu called out again: 'Koona! Koona!'

Even though the rumbling continued, Koona was able to hear him.

'What do you want?' she said irritably.

'We are afraid,' Premu said.

'We are afraid, too,' Koona admitted. 'I'm going to eat my piece of jaggery. I am hungry.' She reached with her left hand for the jaggery in her frock pocket and began to nibble on it. 'Eat some jaggery,' she said to Bolu.

He mumbled to Koona, 'Hold the rope tight. Don't let your grip slacken.'

Koona became so occupied with gripping the rope that she loosened her hold on the jaggery. It slipped out of her hand. 'My jaggery!' she cried.

17

Everyone knew that a rock dropped from the mouth of the hole in the mountain fell at least seven days. People did not know what the maximum depth might be. Perhaps a great-grandfather knew. Some children jumped right over the hole. None of them, not even the children who couldn't jump over the hole, fell in.

Each person could hear the sound of a rock they dropped into the hole. But if someone fell in, they would not be able to return to the mouth to hear themselves dropping down. They would be engrossed in their own falling and continue to fall. They would fall all the time they were alive. They would continue falling even after they had died. 'What happened to them?' someone might ask. 'We don't know. They've been falling for so long we don't know whether they are alive or dead,' someone else might reply.

What if somebody pushed another person into the hole? Would the person who pushed be able to hear the other person falling down? Let's say Bhaira pushed Bolu into the hole. He might return to the hole seven days later to hear Bolu still falling, or might return much later, with the thought that a long time had elapsed and it might be interesting to hear

Bolu's fall. But half-way to the hole, Bhaira might change his mind and never return to the hole again.

There were many people who had dropped rocks into the hole and not returned to the hole for many days. The rocks hadn't stopped dropping for that reason. In fact, the number of rocks that were dropping kept growing. It was possible that one day there would be a fair of people who were returning to hear the descent of their rocks. The fair would come to an end when all the rocks stopped falling. At present, only one or two people returned to listen on a given day. Upon their arrival, one or two rocks would separate from the rest and finish their descent.

The trouble with Bhaira was that he was taken to be deaf when he wasn't so. He refused to hear. What would happen if he went to listen to Bolu dropping and refused to hear?

What if Bhaira was holding on to the rope by which Bolu climbed down the hole? What if the rope in question slipped from Bhaira's hand? Technically, would Bhaira be considered to have dropped Bolu in the hole?

There were old people in the village who heard only a little of what was said.

They would hear only one of the seven days of falling. Would that spare the person being dropped from another six days of falling? In such a case, their bruises would be milder. There were some very old people who heard very little of what was said. They would hear only a soft sound, like the sound of a person placing one foot before the other as they stepped forward. The person they were listening to wouldn't fall; he would merely step forward from the mouth of the hole to the bottom.

18

The others grew impatient after Bolu and Koona went into the hole. Chhotu was the next one to hold on to the rope and descend. He spoke in Bolu's voice from within the hole, 'We should all come down now.' Binu and Premu followed Chhotu. Only Bhaira remained outside, trying to release the rope slowly while five people weighed it down. He didn't succeed. The next thing he knew, the pulley was whirring fast and he, too, was riding the rope down the hole.

Some places inside the mountain were as wide as fields. Others tapered to narrow lanes. The friends were travelling through an entire city that was in the process of falling. The friends dropped fast, the city dropped slowly. The houses along the route of their fall went up; the friends went down. The rope shook unexpectedly, causing the little hands of the children to lose their hold. They travelled down the chute of a sideways lane. There was no other way to journey through the great unknown. They passed many open doors. Through one set of doors Koona saw a man sitting on a bed. Bolu saw the man lying down. Bhaira saw the man slumbering. Bhaira began to yawn.

The friends came across a vegetable market as they fell. The market may have accelerated in hopes of attracting new customers. Once it became clear these were not customers, the vegetable market resumed its slower descent while the friends sped down.

Bolu felt hungry. The friends were separated from one another. They would have held hands if they were closer. Probably they all felt hungry, but for now they were separated and on their own.

Would they have to stay hungry seven days if they fell for seven days? A house dropping slowly to the left of Bolu picked up speed to keep pace with him. A door opened. Two girls stood in the doorway, one older, one younger. The older girl reached out and pulled Bolu into the house.

'Are you hungry?' the younger girl asked him.

'Yes,' Bolu said, stepping inside.

He sat and ate while the younger girl talked non-stop about this and that.

'Can you stay here?' the older girl asked. 'Why don't you stay with us for seven days?'

Bolu noticed an open window across the hall. What looked like rain turned out to be a shower of stones. This was the usual view from the window. Sometimes the shower was strong, sometimes weak. Sometimes it was a mere sprinkle.

The older girl followed Bolu's gaze. She put her

hand out of the window and caught a red-coloured stone as it fell. She was careful to draw her hand back before other stones hit it. Bolu had finished eating.

The stone was round and shiny, smoothed down by years of falling. The older girl handed the stone to Bolu. He turned it this way and that. How could he find out if this was a stone he had tossed into the hole? If only the stone would tell him who had tossed it, where that person lived, and how he or she had felt about tossing the stone. The stone seemed to be slipping out of his hand. Was it anxious over being late? But the stone had not stopped its falling. It continued to fall, like the city that was falling, inhabited by people who were falling, whose ancestors had been falling, whose falling could no longer be heard because everything was falling together.

The older girl took the stone from Bolu and placed it near where it had been falling before. The stone rolled around and found its own place. The scene outside the window frame seemed to have been hung there like a picture. The empty space awaited the stone's return. Once the stone was in place, the entire picture dropped below them.

What would the stone have done if the person who tossed it came to the hole while Bolu held the stone in his hand? How could the stone drop then? How could the 'clink' of its hitting the bottom be produced? Would the stone fly from Bolu's hand and race to the bottom?

Bolu felt satisfied with his meal. 'We have everything in our neighbourhood,' the older girl said. 'The school is not far from the house. You could enroll there.'

'I should be leaving,' Bolu said.

'I'll come with you,' the younger girl said, but her older sister checked her.

'Is your name Bolu?' the older sister asked. 'We've heard of you.'

'My name is Bolu.' He wondered how they could know about him.

By then Bolu had stepped down to the fast-moving narrow lane. He glanced around as he travelled down. He thought the house he had just emerged from might be accompanying him down. Then he remembered the door to the house closing the instant he stepped out. He must have dropped far below. The house was not in view.

Koona had been the first to enter the mouth of the hole and she remained ahead in falling. She looked everywhere as she fell, hoping to find anyone or anything she recognized. She was hungry. As her hunger pangs grew, she noticed a house with a yellow door off to one side. The house adjusted its speed to Koona's falling. There was a white crane sitting on the roof. Except for the yellow door, the house was blue.

Koona stared as the white crane extended its wings and started to climb. Would the crane be able to fly out of the hole? Nothing had been seen to emerge from the hole till now, not even an ant. The yellow door opened and a boy ran out. He wore a blue shirt. He pointed to Koona. The boy's mother picked him up and sat him on her hip.

'How did you find your way to our lane?' the child's mother asked.

'We are celebrating vacation day. We've come here because we have to appear for the vacation day examinations,' Koona replied. 'I'm very hungry,' she added.

'Take my hand.'

The child was on the left hip. The mother extended her right hand to Koona.

The little boy, too, extended his hand.

His mother pulled Koona in.

'How did you travel here?'

'By falling.'

'How will you go from here?'

'I will just disappear,' Koona said.

The boy's mother smiled. 'Wash your hands and have some food. If everything is falling at the same time, it must appear that things are still. Does it appear to you that you are falling?'

Koona raised her right foot. She balanced on her other foot to see if she was steady or falling.

She played with the child when she had finished eating.

Then she remembered the others.

'I am going now,' she said to the child's mother. 'I have lots to do.'

'Come again,' the mother said. She added after a pause, 'But how will you find your way here?'

'Just as I did this time.'

'Come by the front door then. The front door is also painted yellow.'

'There was a crane sitting on your roof that flew away. Are creatures that fly still falling?'

'The crane was falling,' the mother said, 'while it sat on the roof. It was flying when it flew.'

'I'll write to you. Can you give me your address?'

'What address can I give you?'

'Could I send it to The Yellow Door?'

'Yes. That should work.'

'I'll drop the letter into the mouth of the hole in the mountain.'

'I'll write to you, too,' the young boy's mother said. The mother had liked talking to Koona.

'But the door to my house is plain wood without paint.'

'Plain Wood Without Paint is a good address.'

'All right,' Koona said.

Koona had entered by the back door. She had been travelling along the back lane.

'We see many cranes around here. There's a pond in front of the house,' the boy's mother said.

'Is the pond also falling?'

'The entire village is falling, together with its lanes and the pond. We bathe in the pond and wash our clothes there. The pond remains situated in the front of the house. The lane in the back falls faster for some reason. We avoid using the back lane. If someone enters that lane by mistake, they wait till a house appears. They walk through the house and come back to their own home the front way.'

Koona had enjoyed her meal. The others, too, must have chanced upon food, she thought. Just when they felt hungry, a door would have opened. Someone would have invited them in for a meal. They would have gone in through the door. Those who could not leave began dwelling in the houses they entered. The village would have forgotten that their ancestors had arrived by falling. The elders would have established the village generation upon generation ago. Bolu and his friends belonged to a village that had not yet started to fall.

When the rope slipped from his hand Bhaira grew afraid that he would die.

He liked the cool air flowing below. He felt drowsy. He thought that people fell asleep on their way to death. If they woke up, they got to be alive. If they didn't wake up, they slept forever. Bhaira fell asleep as he fell. He turned cartwheels as he fell. He turned on his side. He had dreams of flying. He dreamt he was turning cartwheels as he flew, when in reality he was turning cartwheels as he fell. He was lying in a curl of air inside a well of emptiness.

19

Bolu felt his wind-gust wings extending after he had eaten his fill. He could hear the chaffing of patrangi birds. He had grown so light he no longer fell. He thought his substance had turned into air. Just then a sharp wind, like a broken-off piece from a typhoon, lifted him from below. He kept climbing till he was at the mouth of the hole. Did he travel via a shortcut that brought him up in a jiffy? He knocked the pulley out of the way. It went clattering down the slope. His first thought when he emerged from the hole was for his friends, who must still be on their downward journey within the mountain.

He was aware he didn't have much time. He went straight to the rope maker.

There was a two-days-and-one-night rope hanging from the maulsari tree. Most of its length ran below the ground. Bolu hadn't noticed this rope hanging down when he came out of the hole.

Bolu walked in a circle around the old rope maker and told him about the dilemma he was in. 'What shall I do, Father?' Bolu asked the old man. His innocence in asking the question was as wide as the old man's wisdom was deep.

'It's difficult for me to advise you, son,' the old

man said. 'My special skill is to hear very soft sounds as if they were loud. Why don't you go to Elder Brother, who strolls all the time from the past to the future? He is in the present now; you will find him nearby. He hears loud sounds as if they were soft. He hears a star exploding the instant it happens. The stars whose light you see today disappeared for him when they went extinct. Our far-off future is his immediate present. He is friends with our ancestors and keeps getting together with them. He is hard of hearing, it's true, but this is a matter of inclination. He can put off seeing or hearing if he wishes to. He can assume seeing or hearing if he wishes to. He can see and hear the explosion of a star once, or see the same explosion many times over. Some people say he was present at the nativity of stars. They say many stars are his friends from when they were children. He may not be that old in years but he can travel across billions of years. He can see the light from a star's collapse the moment the star is born.'

Bolu turned these ideas over in his mind as he walked to the Elder Brother's house. The entire house consisted of a single door, as if a door had been planted before the infinite. The door was open. In fact, there was no way of closing it. A person encountered the infinite whichever way they went, whether through the door or by its left or right. The only difference was that going through the door made for happiness. It felt like arriving at a dear person's place filled with the comforts of home.

As soon as Bolu went through the door, he saw the pygmy mountain.

Elder Brother spoke before Bolu could form his words. 'I know,' he said.

He spoke very softly. If Bolu had spoken first, would he have been able to hear the old man's response from four paces away? But it was also true that the old man's voice would sound equally soft and audible if he stood far away. Hearing him from afar was no different from hearing him from near.

Elder Brother gazed into the hole and heard each person dropping to the bottom. He had the right to hear these sounds. The right comes from the love we bear one another. The sound of their dropping was soft, as if they had hadn't really fallen. They were each standing at their ease at the bottom. The individual sounds of their landing sounded like coins. Bhaira must have been the last to land.

He had slumbered peacefully as he fell. The gentle impact woke him.

20

Bolu could hear them shouting. Something came to mind and he stepped out of Elder Brother's house. Even after going through the door, he was where he had been before. Elder Brother was no longer on the pygmy mountain. Was he still inside his house? Had he set out in some other direction? Bolu looked everywhere. Elder Brother seemed to have left simultaneously in every direction. He must have gathered the directions into himself as he left.

They were celebrating. The friends had returned having suffered nothing but a gentle fall at the bottom of the hole. Bolu could hear coins clinking in their pockets as they approached.

Koona reached for Bolu's hand. Her other hand was full of coins. They had all picked up coins from the bottom. Bhaira picked up the most.

Bolu sang:

> Vacation day is ending soon,
> A little time remains.
> Let's toss our coins in the hole,
> Return to hear them fall.
> Our gain will not be someone's loss
> We will return them all.

Koona wanted to give Bolu some of her coins to toss into the hole. Bolu approached the hole but he did not take Koona's coins. She held on to his hand. He said a stone was what he wanted to toss in. He stood at the mouth of the hole. Bhaira selected a smooth stone for Bolu but Bolu picked up a rough, jagged stone and threw it into the hole. The stone would become smooth and shiny from travelling. It might become gold and shiny or blue and shiny. May it be seen as an all-the-time falling stone among the other stones in the frame the window made. Or else, may it be seen as a single stone resting in the alcove of the scene the window made. May the girl recognize the stone as Bolu's. May she reach for the stone and turn it over in her hand before setting it back where it was before. May the stone return to the frame of its falling. Koona wanted that some of the coins her friends dropped would clink on the doorstep of the house with the yellow door. Other friends imagined other routes for their coins.

They couldn't figure out what time it was. They thought vacation day wasn't over. Then they thought it was morning of the next day; they needed to go home and get ready for school. They had to report to Guruji on how they had spent their vacation day.

They were hungry. They found themselves, each of them, standing before the door to their individual houses.

Ten Plain Poems

Vinod Kumar Shukla
Translated from the Hindi by
Satti Khanna

P.S.

Insights
Interviews
& More...

Ten Plain Poems
Vinod Kumar Shukla
Translated from the Hindi by Satti Khanna

1

Once she's out
The house is not on her mind
Once she is in
Outside is not on her mind.

The outside in
The inside out
The inside in
The outside out.

She's sometimes in
She's sometimes out.

2

Such a mass of Rathi cows
All of them identical twins
Herd swelled large from many strays
Cowherd's loss is cow herd's gain.

How to tell the one that strayed
From the others all alike?

Best to take one
And come home.
Was it ours?
Can't be known.

3

Who was that person
Who lived here once?
Which village did he come from?
Where did he go?

He appeared one day
And stayed for a time.
He'll appear again
In some village for a time.

For a time in some village
Someone still thought of him,
Someone forgot him.

4

'That's where I want to go.
'Where would that be?' Mother inquires.
'There.'
'Tell us where there is,' they ask.
'There!' says the daughter.
'There!'

'Let's set out,' they say.
'Her there may lie along the way.'

They start walking.

The daughter follows,
Stopping along the way
To spin in place.

Comes home contented.

5

Having learned to count to a hundred (1)

Now she wanted to count the stars,
Countless stars
Filling the sky.

She counted to seventy-nine,
The other numbers she forgot.

Not making a hundred—
Poor countless stars.

6

Having learned to count to a hundred (2)

'A tiger lived in a forest,'
Mother began.
'Only one?'
The daughter asked.

Easier to count birds in flight
Than tigers taking cover
In the underbrush.

One tiger's as good as another
Count one tiger
Count them all.
The one tiger was counted
Here and there
A hundred times.

Mother told the story
Of a tiger that lived in a forest
A hundred times.

7

I'm not going out there to play
Wherever the others have gone.
I'll stay here alone.

Play the game of staying here
Till they're done and come back home.
I don't know where they have gone
To play the games we like to play.

I'll stay here alone
Play the game of staying here.

8

The little choo-choo engine
Of Siya dozing off
The single household wagon
Heavy with sleep.

An elephant crossed the tracks
Siya started from her dream
Someone pulled the chain
The train lurched to a stop.

'What happened to Siya?'
'What's gone wrong?'

9

She's so lovely, everyone says.
So, so lovely, everyone says.

How lovely would that be then?

So, so lovely.

So, so lovely.

10

Messed up map
Slanting seas
Oxbow rivers
Islands creased.

Zigzag sky
Taking up room
Horizons awry
Directions confused.

Crammed Infinite here
Spread Infinite there.

'The work of a child,'
A sadhu declares.